Jane opened her mouth to speak and then closed it again.

Without her shoes she had even further to look up into the professor's face, but there was nothing in it to indicate if she had dreamt his words—perhaps he was joking . . .

'What did you say?'

'I asked you to marry me.' He smiled gently down at her. 'Believe me, I have given the matter some thought and I consider it to be a most suitable arrangement. The best thing is for you to marry me.'

Dear Reader

This month, I would like to ask you to think about the kind of heroine you would like to find in our stories. Do you think she should be sweet and gentle, on the look-out for a man who will be able to care for and nurture her, or should the heroine be able to give as good as she gets, throwing punch for punch, and quite capable of standing up for herself? If you have any opinions on this matter please let us know, so that we can continue to give you the books you want to read!

The Editor

Betty Neels spent her childhood and youth in Devonshire before training as a nurse and midwife. She was an army nursing sister during the war, married a Dutchman, and subsequently lived in Holland for fourteen years. She lives with her husband in Dorset, and has a daughter and grandson. Her hobbies are reading, animals—she owns a matronly Moggy—old buildings and writing. Betty started to write on retirement from nursing, incited by a lady in a library bemoaning the lack of romantic novels.

Recent titles by the same author:

A HAPPY MEETING
THE QUIET PROFESSOR
AN OLD-FASHIONED GIRL
A GIRL IN A MILLION

AT ODDS
WITH LOVE

BY

BETTY NEELS

MILLS & BOON LIMITED
ETON HOUSE, 18-24 PARADISE ROAD
RICHMOND, SURREY TW9 1SR

First published in Great Britain 1993 by Mills & Boon Limited

© Betty Neels 1993

Australian copyright 1993 Philippine copyright 1993 This edition 1993

ISBN 0 263 78169 0

Set in Times Roman 10½ on 12 pt. 01-9308-53486 C

Made and printed in Great Britain

CHAPTER ONE

THE October afternoon was drawing to a misty close and the last rays of the sun, shining through the latticed window, highlighted the russet hair of the young woman sitting by it. It shone upon her lovely face too and gave her green eyes an added sparkle as she stared out at the garden beyond, the knitting in her lap forgotten for the moment.

It was quiet in the room save for the faint ticking of the clock on the mantelpiece and the sighing breaths of the old lady in the bed as she dozed. It was a pleasant room, low-ceilinged, its walls papered in an old-fashioned pattern of flowers, the furniture for the most part ponderous Victorian; the small person in the bed was dwarfed by her surroundings, perched up against her pillows. She stirred presently and the girl got up and went to the bedside.

'You've had a nice nap, Granny. If you're quite comfortable I'll go and get the tea-tray.' She had a charming voice and she spoke cheerfully. 'I'll light a lamp, shall I?' And when the old lady nodded, she added, 'It's a beautiful evening—I do love this time of year.'

The old lady smiled and nodded again and the girl went away, down to the kitchen of the rambling old house where Bessy the housekeeper was making the tea. She looked up as the girl went in.

''Ad a nap, 'as she? The dear soul—wore out, she must be.' She put a plate of wafer-thin bread and butter on the tray. 'And time you 'as a bit of fresh air, Miss Jane. I'll sit with 'er while you take a turn round the garden when you've had your tea.'

Jane leaned across the table and cut a slice of bread, buttered it lavishly and said thickly through a mouthful, 'Thank you, Bessy. I'll take Bruno and Percy and Simpkin with me—just for ten minutes or so.'

She gobbled up the rest of her bread and butter and picked up the tray. She was a tall girl with a splendid shape, dressed rather carelessly in a cotton blouse, a well-worn cardigan and a long wide skirt.

The housekeeper eyed her as she went to the door. 'You didn't ought ter look so shabby.' She spoke with the freedom of an old and faithful servant. 'Suppose some nice young man should call?'

Jane gave a gurgle of laughter and Bessy said severely, 'Well, you may laugh, Miss Jane, but there's Dr Willoughby coming regular to see your granny.'

'He is an engaged man, Bessy, and several inches shorter than I am.'

She went back upstairs to heave the old lady gently up against her pillows and give her her tea. She would eat nothing, though, and Jane thought that she looked paler than usual.

'Feel all right, Granny?' she asked casually.

'A little tired, dear. Have you seen to Bruno and the cats?'

'I'm going to take them into the garden presently and give them their supper. They're all splendid.' She added in what she hoped sounded like an after-thought, 'Dr Willoughby might be coming this evening instead of tomorrow . . .'

'A nice young man. A pity he's going to marry. He would have done very well for you, Jane. You're twenty-seven and you've given up a good nursing career to look after me here, buried in the country.'

'I like being here,' protested her granddaughter. 'I like the country and I haven't met a man I want to marry yet.'

'Though you've had your chances...?'

'Well, yes, I dare say I'm fussy.' She rearranged the pillows as Bessy came into the room. 'There now— I'm off to see to the animals.'

Only when she got downstairs she went to the phone first and dialled Dr Willoughby and asked him to come and see her grandmother. 'I don't think she's any worse, but I'm uneasy...'

She saw to the cats and Bruno next. Bruno was a corgi and the cats were both ginger, one middle-aged and dignified and the other much younger, with eyes as green as Jane's and a thick ruff of fur under his chin. They all paced round the large garden in the gloom and presently went indoors to settle before the fire in the small sitting-room Jane used now that her grandmother was no longer able to come downstairs and use the big drawing-room. She had just settled them, piled companionably into one basket, when the doctor arrived and she took him upstairs.

He was a youngish man with a large country practice and he had been looking after Mrs Wesley since she first became ill. He greeted her easily and, previously prompted by Jane, observed that he had a busy day on the morrow, and, since he was passing, he had decided to pay her a visit.

He didn't stay long but checked her pulse and examined her chest as he always did, bade her a cheerful goodnight and asked Jane to go down with him. 'I have some pills which will help your breathing,' he explained.

'You were quite right,' he told Jane as she ushered him into the sitting-room. 'Mrs Wesley isn't so well and I suspect a small pulmonary embolism. Will you allow me to call in a specialist? Nowadays it is possible to operate and remove the clot—I know it's a grave risk because of your grandmother's age, but at least we shall have taken the best advice possible.'

'Oh, please—do whatever you think is best. Can he come quickly, this specialist?'

'He's a busy man but I have met him—he was already making a name for himself when I was a houseman. He's not always in this country, though. I'll try and get hold of him this evening and let you know. Meanwhile, you know what to do for your grandmother and please don't hesitate to phone if you're worried.'

He went away, leaving Jane standing in the charming room with its slightly shabby brocade curtains and graceful Regency furniture. After a moment or two she went back upstairs, remarking as she went into Mrs Wesley's room, 'Shall I read to you? What do you feel like? Something soothing or one of your whodunnits?'

Her grandmother chuckled, a whisper of sound hardly to be heard. 'Shall we have Trollope? I suspect Dr Willoughby wouldn't want me to get too excited.'

'*Phineas Finn . . .*'

It was after Mrs Wesley had been settled for the night and the house was quiet that Dr Willoughby phoned. 'We shall be with you tomorrow around midday. He's a good man, the best—rest assured, if there's anything that can be done he'll do it.'

They came the next morning and Jane, as a slight concession to the consultant's visit—for she was sure that he was a worthy man and no doubt aware of that worth—put on a blue cotton sweater over a darker blue denim skirt. She would have put her abundant hair up, only her grandmother needed more attention than usual and there wasn't time, so she brushed it hard and tied it back.

'At least you're tidy,' grumbled Bessy, 'not but what you look half your age.'

'Oh, Bessy, what does it matter how I look, if only they can do something for Granny?'

She heard Dr Willoughby's rather elderly Ford coming along the drive to the house as she was putting the finishing touches to Mrs Wesley's hair; ill she might be, but the old lady still had her small vanities.

They came up the old uncarpeted staircase unhurriedly with Bessy ahead of them to open the door and usher them in, and Jane looked up expectantly. She hadn't been sure what to expect but her expectations had been coloured by the various consultants at the hospital where she had been a ward sister: older men, dignified and a little remote, made so by the knowledge that they had crammed into their heads over the years. This man, towering beside Dr Willoughby, didn't tally with her guess; he was still young, not yet forty, she judged, a giant of a man and heavily built. He was good-looking, too, with a high arched nose and a thin mouth above a determined chin, and when he was introduced as Professor van der Vollenhove he offered a large cool hand, and looked at her briefly from eyes the colour of a winter sea, pale and cold, and indifferent to her.

With her grandmother, however, it was an entirely different matter. He sat down beside her bed and talked to her in a slow, slightly accented voice and presently he set about examining her. Dr Willoughby had gone to stand by the window, and Jane, by the bed, ready to do whatever was asked of her, had ample opportunity to study the professor at close quarters.

His suit was superbly tailored, she noticed, his linen pristine, the gold cufflinks plain. She was pleased that there was no sign of baldness in his thick grizzled hair; it must have been very pale brown when he was younger. It pleased her when he said something to make her grandmother chuckle weakly and he laughed himself. He was probably quite nice when one got to know him.

She eased Mrs Wesley into a more comfortable position and stepped back from the bed. The professor was talking in a quiet voice and she couldn't hear all that he was saying, but he sounded reassuring without being hearty and her grandmother looked cheerful.

They shook hands presently, his large one engulfing her small bony one very gently, and then he got up. 'You are in very capable hands,' he observed. 'Dr Willoughby and I will have a talk and probably try out some further treatment. I will come and see you again if I may?'

Jane saw the hope in her grandmother's pale little face. 'Please do. Jane will get you coffee downstairs.' She turned to look at her. 'Run along, dear, and look after the gentlemen. I should like to rest for a little while.'

Jane led the way downstairs, ushered the two men into the drawing-room where Bessy had lighted a fire and went along to the kitchen. In answer to the housekeeper's look she said, 'They haven't told me anything yet, Bessy. I'll tell you when they do. I'll take the tray in—you pop up and make sure Granny's all right, will you?'

She poured the coffee from the silver coffee-pot into the delicate china cups and handed the shortbread she had made the previous evening. It was only when she had seated herself without fuss that anyone spoke.

The professor put down his cup. 'As Dr Willoughby rightly suspected, Mrs Wesley has a small pulmonary embolism. In a young person I would advise operation, a serious matter as you no doubt know, but your grandmother is an old lady and very weak and I cannot advise that. I am sorry to tell you that there is nothing much to be done other than to see that she is free from pain. She is likely to die suddenly and soon.' He added gravely, 'I am so sorry to have to tell you this.'

Jane's cup rattled in its saucer but her voice was steady. 'Thank you for being frank, Professor van der Vollenhove. I'm sure if there was a chance you would take it.' She looked at them both. 'You will make sure that Granny is as comfortable as possible?' She stopped to swallow the lump in her throat. 'She is a very brave person.'

'Rest assured of that.' The professor sounded kind and she had no doubt that he was to be trusted. She wondered fleetingly what he was like—the man behind the perfection of his professional manner. She remembered the coldness of his eyes when they had met, not so much dislike as indifference. Not that it mattered; held firmly at the back of her mind was the knowledge that her grandmother was going to die, to be held at bay until she would be free to give way to her grief. Meanwhile, life would go on as usual and she would do everything she could to keep the old lady happy.

She listened carefully to the two men debating what was best to be done and presently the professor wrote out a prescription. 'This won't make your grandmother drowsy or prevent her from enjoying her daily routine, but it will keep her calm and unworried. Discontinue everything else.'

'Will you come again?'

'I am at your disposal should I be needed.' She got up and he shook her hand. Looking up into his face, she saw that his eyes were a clear light blue and his glance serious. She thanked him gravely and saw them both to the door.

'I'll be round this evening,' Dr Willoughby promised. 'You know you can phone me at any time.'

She watched the car go down the drive and turn into the lane beyond and then she went in search of Bessy.

The housekeeper was washing up the coffee-cups. 'Bad news, Miss Jane?'

Jane told her. Bessy had been with her grandmother for a very long time; Jane remembered her from when she had been sent as a child to stay with her grandmother while her parents were abroad, and she was as much a family friend as a housekeeper. 'And I must phone Basil...'

Basil was Jane's only other relation, a cousin, an orphan like herself, but that was all they had in common. They had never liked each other as children and now they were adults they saw very little of each other. He was older than she was by a year or two and would eventually inherit his grandmother's house and possessions. He was making his career in banking and hadn't been to see Mrs Wesley for a long time. When she rang him presently it was apparent that he had no intention of doing so now.

'Let me know how the old lady is,' he told her. 'I can't possibly get away, and I doubt if she knows who I am anyway.' He rang off before she could say anything else.

It was three days later, as Jane was reading the last few pages of *Phineas Finn*, that her grandmother said softly, 'Basil will look after you, my dear,' and died as gently and quietly as she had lived.

There was a great deal to do; Jane got on with it, holding her grief in check, time enough for that when everything which had to be done was done. Basil, when told, said that he would come for the funeral and made no offer of help, not that she had expected him to. Dr Willoughby was a tower of strength and Bessy, tight-lipped and red-eyed, saw to it that some sort of a normal routine was maintained.

Mrs Wesley had had many friends—the village church was full and after the service those who knew her well went back to the house. Jane, circulating with plates of sandwiches and offers of coffee or tea, saw that Basil had already assumed the air of master of the house. Presently, when everyone had gone and Mr Chepstow, their solicitor, had taken a seat in the sitting-room, he followed her into the kitchen where she had gone with a tray of plates. 'You'd better come, I suppose,' he told her. 'Old Chepstow seems to think you should be there.' He turned to Bessy. 'And you—whatever your name is—you are to come too.'

'This is Bessy, grandmother's housekeeper,' said Jane coldly. 'She has looked after her for years.'

He shrugged and turned away and they followed him back to the sitting-room where Mr Chepstow was toasting himself before the small bright fire.

'Well, shall we get started? I must get back to town this evening—I've an important meeting . . .'

Mr Chepstow wasn't to be hurried. He read the will slowly and Jane was pleased to hear that Bessy was to have a small pension for the rest of her life; she herself was to receive five hundred pounds with the wish that her cousin Basil would take upon himself the duty of giving her a home for as long as she wanted it, and making such financial provision for her as he deemed fitting. The estate was left entirely to him.

Mr Chepstow folded the will carefully and stood up. 'You will wish to make financial arrangements, no doubt,' he told Basil. 'If you care to make an appointment when it is convenient to you, I will be pleased to deal with anything you may have in mind.'

Basil wasn't listening; he nodded impatiently and bustled the solicitor out to his waiting taxi and then came back into the house.

'I've no time now,' he told Jane. 'I'll be back in a day or two.'

His goodbye was perfunctory and he was gone, driving away in his flashy car.

''E didn't ask if we 'ad any money,' observed Bessy tartly. ''E may be yer cousin, Miss Jane, but I don't like 'im.' She picked up the poker and bashed the logs in the grate. 'And 'e don't need ter think I'll be staying—not for 'im—there's me sister in Stepney, got a nice little 'ouse now she's widdered—me and me pension will be more than welcome...'

She glanced at Jane sitting composedly by the fire. 'And you, Miss Jane, what about you?'

'I'll go back to nursing, Bessy. It may take a few weeks to get a job but I can stay here. There are Bruno and Percy and Simpkin to think of too. I must try and find homes for them, although Basil might take them over.'

''E might, and then again 'e might not. You can ask 'im when 'e comes again.'

Jane was kept busy for the next few days; there were letters to write and answer, friends calling, small household bills to be paid and their own modest needs to be dealt with. She kept a careful account of the money she spent and wondered what she was to do once the housekeeping purse was empty. She had a little money of her own but she hadn't earned any for the last few months and it might be a month or more before she would get a pay packet. While she pondered her future she did her best to keep her sorrow at bay. She would go as soon as possible, she reflected; there were plenty of large provincial hospitals and she knew that she would get an excellent reference from the London hospital she had left when she'd come to look after her grandmother. She knew that Basil didn't like her over-much but it was unlikely that he would want to come and live in the house immediately. She was never quite sure what he did in the city; if it was a high-powered job then he might commute at weekends as so many of her grandmother's neighbours did and the will had stipulated that he should give her a home as long as she needed one and financial help too. The latter she had no intention of accepting if it were offered; she was quite capable of supporting herself, but it would be nice if he allowed her to stay sometimes . . .

She and Bessy cleaned and polished the house and tidied the flowerbeds, already touched with the first autumn frosts, and waited for Basil to return.

He came at the end of a week, and not alone this time. Jane, watching from the drawing-room window where she had been arranging a bowl of chrysanthemums on the rent table, saw him help a girl out of the car; a small slim creature with a cloud of dark hair and dressed unsuitably for the country, although the black and white striped suit she was wearing was the last word in fashion. Even at that distance Jane felt a surge of dislike. I am becoming a spiteful old maid, she reflected as she went to open the door.

'Hello,' said Basil. 'This is Myra, my fiancée. Darling, this is Jane, my cousin, remember?'

Myra wasn't a girl, she was a woman, older than Jane, exquisitely turned out and very sure of herself. She said, 'Oh, hello, Jane, Basil's brought me to see the house. I dare say it needs a good deal of refurbishing—old, isn't it?'

'Two hundred years or so,' said Jane drily. 'Do come in.'

Basil threw her a dagger glance which she ignored; it was still her home until he asked her to leave. 'I'm sure you would like coffee. I'll make some—there's a fire in the drawing-room. We light it once or twice a week to keep the room aired.'

'We'll start looking round,' said Basil, 'we haven't got all day. Let us know when the coffee is ready.'

He swept Myra out of the room and across the hall into the dining-room and Jane, speechless at his rudeness, flounced along to the kitchen where she vented her ill humour on the cups and saucers.

'What's bitten you?' asked Bessy, coming in with a pile of washing. 'Smashing round like a bull in a china shop.'

'Basil's here,' said Jane between her teeth. 'He's brought his fiancée; they're touring the house. They can have instant coffee and those biscuits I made yesterday.'

She bore the tray away presently and went in search of Basil and Myra. They were in her grandmother's bedroom. 'We'll throw this stuff out for a start,' Myra was saying, and looked over her shoulder as Jane went in.

'It's large enough,' she conceded, 'but some of the furniture is pretty out of date . . .'

'Most of it is antique.' She looked at Basil and added, 'And quite valuable, I understand.'

'Well, that's for me to decide now. Is that coffee ready?'

'In the drawing-room, if you'd like to come downstairs.'

Seething with rage though she was, Jane didn't allow it to show; she handed the coffee and biscuits with perfect civility and made polite conversation.

'Aren't you bored here?' asked Myra. 'It must have been dull living here with an old lady.'

'She was my grandmother,' Jane replied tartly. 'She was Basil's too, you know. I like the country.'

'Don't you like living in London?' asked Myra curiously.

'I had friends there and a good job but I came here when I had weekends or holidays.'

Basil said suddenly, 'Well, you'll miss that. You've had your fair share of living in comfort here; you won't be able to get round us the way you got round Grandmother. Myra and I are to be married within the next week or so, and we shall be living here. I suppose you'll have to stay a few days longer to pack up your things—you can go and stay with some of those friends of yours,' he added with a sneer. 'And that woman in the kitchen, she can go too.' His eye lighted on the basket under the rent table. 'That dog and the cats—two of them? I'll get the vet to collect them, they can be put down.'

Jane stared at him, willing herself not to speak until she could control her tongue. 'In Grandmother's will,' she reminded him as soon as she could trust her voice, 'she asked if I might regard this as home; I see now that that isn't possible and I'm sure that if she had known that you intended marrying she wouldn't have wanted that—I certainly don't. Nor do I want any financial help from you, not that you're likely to offer it, are you? She did, however, ask that the animals should be cared for. At least give me time to find homes for them.'

He laughed. 'Well, I am taking care of them, aren't I? And you're right, Jane, I have no intention of doing anything for you; you can earn your own living any way you like. Find yourself a husband if you can, though with that sharp tongue of yours I doubt if you'll succeed. I'll be back in two days' time. That woman who looks after the place can stay until I get new staff but you will go, you and the dog and cats.' He got up. 'Come along, darling, we'll go back to town and get hold of a good interior decorator. He can get started by the end of the week and we can live in part of the house until he's finished.'

They went to the door and Myra lingered for a moment. 'You shouldn't have much trouble finding a man,' she observed kindly. 'Doctors mostly marry nurses, don't they? Nice meeting you.'

Jane stood on the steps outside the door for a long time making a great effort to get calm so that she could explain it all to Bessy. Presently she went along to the kitchen. The postman was there, drinking the mug of tea the housekeeper had poured for him and Jane said, 'No, don't get up, Jimmy, I'll have a mug too, if I may, Bessy. Any letters?'

A handful for her and one for Bessy which she was reading.

'Well, I never—that Mr Chepstow wants ter see me as soon as possible. Well, it'll have ter be tomorror—the bus went 'alf an 'our ago.'

'Give you a lift?' offered Jimmy.

'Well, I dunno—'as Mr Basil gone?'

'Yes, Bessy, you go—you'll be able to catch the afternoon bus back. You look fine—get your coat and hat while Jimmy finishes his tea.'

The house was very quiet when they had gone away in Jimmy's van; Blandford wasn't far and although Mr Chepstow hadn't given any day or time in his letter surely he would see Bessy. To make sure, Jane picked up the telephone and explained to the solicitor.

'Just a little matter of her signature,' he explained, 'I don't know if she will stay on at the house; if not she will be glad to have the money.'

'She will be leaving,' said Jane. 'Basil is getting married and coming to live here within the next week or so.'

'And you?'

'I shall be going too.'

'Dear, dear, that isn't at all what your dear grand-mother intended. Have you somewhere to go, Jane? And what about a job—can you get your post at the hospital back?'

'Well, no, it's been filled for months, but I shall be quite all right. I'll let you know my address once I'm settled.'

She sounded so confident that he put the phone down with a sigh of relief. It upset him that Basil should disregard his grandmother's wishes but there was nothing much he could do about it and, as it had turned out, there would be no need. Jane, he remembered, had had a ward sister's post for a year or two before she had gone to live with her grandmother, quite a well paid job; she would certainly have sufficient funds to see her through the next week or so; all the same, he would make sure that she had the five hundred pounds as quickly as possible.

Jane tidied the kitchen and went back to the drawing-room. Until now she had done everything in a kind of bad dream but the sight of Bruno sitting before the fire with Percy and Simpkin each side of him turned the dream into reality. She knelt beside them, glad of the warmth of the fire. 'Don't worry, my dears,' she begged them. 'I'll think of something. Not the local kennels; Basil would soon find out about that. There's no one in the village—everyone I know has dogs and cats with no room for more.'

She got up and fetched pen and paper and started to do sums. Boarding them would cost money and she hadn't a great deal; besides, they couldn't stay shut up forever. She could try one of the animal sanctuaries, somewhere where they could all be together. She would have to go back to London and go to an agency and get a job as quickly as possible and then take her time applying for a post at one of the larger hospitals. She would have to pack too... The phone rang and she went to answer it. It was Basil.

'We've stopped for coffee,' he told her, and added, 'And we have just remembered to remind you not to take anything which isn't yours——'

'How dare you?' said Jane and banged down the receiver just as the front doorbell rang.

She had gone pale with rage and flung the door open, not caring who was there or why; it could be a gang of thieves for all she cared.

It was Professor van der Vollenhove, and at the sight of him the unhappiness and misery and fear of the future welled up and choked her. She burst into tears and flung her not inconsiderable person on to his massive chest.

The professor remained calm, a comforting arm around her shoulders, a hand offering a spotless white handkerchief, and, since she seemed incapable of using it, he mopped her wet face. Not that it made much difference; she went on sniffing and sobbing into his waistcoat for some minutes but presently she blew her charming nose and dried her eyes and disentangled herself.

'Oh, I'm so ashamed. Do forgive me, it's just...' A large tear trickled down her cheek. 'He's going to have them put down,' she mumbled, and a second tear started down the other cheek. Despite her pink nose and tear-stained face she still looked lovely. She looked up into his impassive face. 'She loved them...'

He took the sopping handkerchief from her. 'Come inside and tell me about it?' he suggested.

A firm hand between her shoulderblades urging her on, Jane led him into the drawing-room. She said on a watery hiccup, 'So sorry—if you will sit down I'll make some coffee.'

For answer he swept her into a chair and sat down opposite her, his long legs stretched out before him, the epitome of relaxation—something the animals must have sensed, for they came to look up into his face and then sat themselves tidily at his feet.

'I have a call to make fairly near here; I came to offer my condolences. I was sorry to hear about Mrs Wesley, a charming and brave old lady.' When Jane nodded he said, 'Begin at the beginning and tell me what has gone wrong.'

He was the last person she would have confided in; she had gained the impression that he hadn't liked her, but now it all came tumbling out, a bit muddled though she made a brave effort to tell him nothing but the facts. Only when she told him about having Bruno and Percy and Simpkin put down did she falter. 'You see,' she added, 'there's nothing to stop Basil—it's all his...' She looked up. 'It's kind of you to listen. I'll go and make the coffee.'

'Let us forget the coffee for the moment.' He sounded coolly friendly. 'I think that I am able to help you.' At her look of delighted relief he said, 'You will as well be helping me and you will get the worst of the bargain. I am on my way to call upon an old friend of my mother: Lady Grimstone—perhaps you know her?'

'Yes—well, Granny did.'

'Then you will know that she is an irascible old lady with an uncertain temper and emphysema. She has had a companion for years—a Miss Smithers—badly in need of a holiday. So far, none of the applicants to replace her for a month has proved suitable. You might do.' He smiled thinly. 'It needs to be someone who needs work badly; she is extremely difficult. There is one advantage, however—Miss Smithers has two cats and Lady Grimstone has a very old basset hound; I believe she would have no objection to your having these small creatures with you.'

'You mean that, really?'

He gave her a look which chilled the sudden glow of hope welling up in her insides.

'I am not in the habit of speaking lightly, Miss Fox.'

She said hastily, 'No, no, I'm sure you're not, Professor. If you think I might do I'll apply for the post. I'm most grateful...'

'You may regret saying that.' He looked her over in his cool way. 'So now go and do something to your face and hair but show me first where I can make coffee.'

'You'll make the coffee?' Her amazement was transparent.

His faintly mocking look stopped her from saying anything else; she led him to the kitchen, pointed out the coffee-pot, the Aga and the coffee-mill on the wall. Let him do his best, she thought, skimming through the door to her room.

She felt herself again, able to cope, and although she flinched away from the memory of her outburst she had the good sense to know that it was something which sooner or later would have occurred. She washed her face and dashed on some powder and some lipstick, brushed her hair smoothly into a French pleat and searched her wardrobe for something suitable to wear. She chose a cotton chambray dress the colour of clotted cream with a neat collar and shaped yoke and a thick knit cardigan to wear with it, one she had knitted herself while sitting with her grandmother. She hoped that she looked reasonably like a companion as she ran back downstairs to the kitchen and found the professor pouring coffee into two mugs.

He scarcely looked at her. 'I need to be back in town by four o'clock,' he observed and handed her a mug.

'I don't suppose Lady Grimstone will take very long interviewing me,' ventured Jane.

'Probably not; we should be away from there in plenty of time. I'll drop you off here as I go.'

'Won't that take you out of your way?'

'No. I can take the A354 to Salisbury and pick up the A303.' His tone made it plain that it wasn't her concern. She drank her coffee and told him meekly that she was ready if he wanted to leave.

CHAPTER TWO

LADY GRIMSTONE lived on the outskirts of a hamlet away from the road between Pimperne and Tarrant Hinton, not many miles from Mrs Wesley's house as a crow might fly, but by car it meant taking the lane through the village and on until it joined the main road to Blandford and then taking another side-road, to finally turn off into a narrow lane.

Jane had been momentarily diverted from her thoughts of an uncertain future by the sight of the Bentley Continental outside the door. Understated elegance, she reflected, admiring its sober dark grey and the soft leather of its interior. If she had known the professor better, or been more certain of his opinion of her, she would have commented on it—as it was, she got in when he opened the door for her and sat serenely beside him. She had found time to leave a note in case Bessy came back first, check that the windows were closed, make sure that she had the keys and that the Aga was smouldering as it should, and assure the animals that she would be back very shortly before she went out of the house to join him. He wasn't to know that she had the urge—strong in all females—to go back and check everything once more before finally closing the door and giving the handle a quick turn just to make sure that it was shut.

They spoke hardly at all as he drove. Jane, the sharp edge of her grief washed away by her tears, pondered her prospects—a month would give her time to apply

25

for as many posts as possible and she had enough money to rent a small flat or even a large bedsitter for a week or two as long as it had a balcony so that the animals could stay easily. She sat debating with herself as to which city would be the best in which to apply for a post, unaware that her companion, glancing at her from time to time, could see her frown and guessed a little of what she was thinking.

'It is just a waste of time to plan your future until you have this job.'

His voice, cool and impersonal, broke into her thoughts.

'You think I might not be suitable?'

'Why should you not be suitable? But you would be wise to take things as they come.'

He was right, of course, even though his advice lacked warmth.

Lady Grimstone lived in a solid country residence set in conventional grounds, a mere half-mile from the village, but the walls round it were high and the double gates were closed so that the professor had to lean on his horn until a flustered woman came from the lodge.

'Lady Grimstone doesn't encourage visitors,' observed the professor drily as he drove along the drive to the house.

A stern-visaged woman admitted them, ushered them into a small room off the hall and went away. Jane sat down composedly; it was no use getting uptight. Things didn't look too promising at the moment but she needed the job and she reminded herself that beggars couldn't be choosers.

The professor, entirely at his ease, had gone to look out of the window; an encouraging word or two would have been kind, she reflected with a touch of peevishness. It was on the tip of her tongue to say so when the door opened and the woman asked them to follow her.

They were led upstairs to a portrait-lined gallery above and ushered in to a room facing the staircase. The room was large and had a balcony overlooking the grounds; it was furnished with a great many tables and uncomfortable-looking chairs, the tables loaded with ornaments and photos in silver frames. The room was also very hot with a fire blazing in the hearth. Sitting by the fire in a high-backed chair was Lady Grimstone, a formidable figure, her stoutness well corseted and clothed in purple velvet—an unfortunate choice, thought Jane, with that high complexion. She looked ill tempered, her mouth turned down at its corners, but as the professor entered the room with Jane beside him she smiled.

'Nikolaas—how delightful to see you. You bring news of your dear mother, no doubt.' She fished the pince-nez from her upholstered bosom. 'And who is this? Do I know her?'

'Miss Jane Fox, who, I hope, will take over from Miss Smithers for a short while. A trained nurse and most competent,' he added smoothly.

Lady Grimstone studied Jane at some length. 'I cannot really understand why Miss Smithers should need a holiday,' she observed. 'She leads a very pleasant life here with me.'

The professor didn't bat an eyelid. 'Oh, undoubtedly, but it is two—three years since she visited her sister in Scotland; a month away doesn't seem unreasonable to me, Lady Grimstone, and besides you will benefit from her fresh outlook when she returns.'

He added suavely, 'We all need to make sacrifices from time to time...'

Lady Grimstone's massive person swelled alarmingly. 'You are right, of course. How like your dear father you are, Nikolaas, and I know that you have my welfare at heart.'

She looked at Jane again. 'I have constant ill health,' she observed. 'My present companion, Miss Smithers, understands my needs; it is to be hoped that you will do your best to emulate her.' She adjusted the pince-nez. 'How old are you?'

'Twenty-seven, Lady Grimstone.'

'And no followers, I trust?'

Without looking at him, Jane knew that Professor van der Vollenhove was amused. 'No.'

'You like animals? I have a dog. Miss Smithers has cats but I presume that they will go with her if and when she goes on holiday.'

'I do like animals; I have two cats and a dog.'

To her surprise Lady Grimstone took the news with equanimity. 'You would have Miss Smithers's room, quite suitable for animals. The dog is small?'

'Yes, Lady Grimstone.'

'Ring the bell, if you please, Nikolaas.'

When the woman answered it she said, 'Tell Miss Smithers to come here,' in a demanding tone without so much as a please.

Miss Smithers came into the room silently, a sensible-looking woman in her forties. She had a pleasant face and a quiet voice.

'You wanted me, Lady Grimstone?'

'As you see, Professor van der Vollenhove has come to see me—his mother is one of my dearest friends. He has found someone to take your place while you go on this holiday. Take her away and explain your duties.'

Miss Smithers didn't answer but smiled at Jane and went to the door and Jane followed. 'Come down to my room,' invited Miss Smithers. 'We can talk there.'

She led the way downstairs and opened a door leading from the hall, ushered Jane through it and closed the door behind her. 'You must need a job badly,' she observed in her sensible voice. She smiled as she spoke and Jane smiled back.

'Oh, I do. You see I have to leave—my home, and I have two cats and a dog. It seemed hopeless but Professor van der Vollenhove called this morning and said he knew of something. Is it a difficult job?'

'No, but you will have no life of your own and you are still so young—for myself it suits well enough; I am able to save money and when I have sufficient I shall retire. I like a quiet life and Lady Grimstone is most lenient about pets and that is important to me— to you too, I expect?'

'Yes, more important than anything else. If I can't find somewhere they will be welcome my cousin will have them put down.'

'Sit down and tell me about it,' invited Miss Smithers.

It was nice to talk to someone who was willing to listen and who, when Jane had finished her sorry little tale, assured her that, difficult though Lady Grimstone was, this was obviously the answer to her prayers. 'I'll tell you the daily routine...'

Her day would start early and finish late but from time to time there would be a chance to have an hour or two to herself, 'And Lady Grimstone expects you to walk her dog several times a day which means you can take yours at the same time. As you can see, this room is ideal——' she crossed the room and opened the glass doors leading to a small conservatory '—it's ideal for cats and dogs. I leave the outside door open so that they can get in and out if I'm not here—there's a high wall right round the garden so they can't go far.'

A bell pinged loudly and Miss Smithers said, 'That's Lady Grimstone now. I must warn you that she rings any time during the twenty-four hours and will expect you to be there within minutes. Do you still want the job? It's for a month...do you know how much you'll be paid?'

'I've no idea, I just want somewhere for a few weeks while I decide what to do—I'm a nurse—I've had a ward for several years, I intend to apply for a job, but it takes time. This is perfect...'

'Can you not stay with your cousin? Would he not allow you to remain for a few weeks?'

Jane, who had glossed over the gloomier aspects of her tale, admitted that she had just two days in which to leave the house. 'So you see, it is urgent.'

'Well, we'll soon see what she's decided.' They went back upstairs to the drawing-room and found Lady Grimstone still in her chair and the professor standing with his back to the fire.

'Professor van der Vollenhove recommends you, Miss Fox, and I dare say you'll do and be no worse than anyone else. He tells me that you're free to come at once so you, Miss Smithers, can pack your bags and be off. A month, mind, not a day more. Have you explained your duties?'

'Yes, Lady Grimstone. May I suggest that I go on the day after tomorrow and that Miss Fox comes tomorrow so that she may see exactly how you like things done?'

'I had already thought of that,' declared Lady Grimstone, who hadn't. 'How will you get here?' she asked abruptly, and Jane thought, Rude old woman; but before she could answer the professor said carelessly, 'Oh, I've another visit to make in Blandford, I can easily collect Miss Fox and her luggage and animals.' He didn't wait for the old lady to reply but asked Jane, 'Will ten o'clock suit you? That will give you all day to find your way around before Miss Smithers goes.'

'Thank you, it's kind of you to offer.'

'Now I'm afraid I must be off and if you're ready, Miss Fox, I'll drop you off—I pass your door.'

Lady Grimstone was pleased to be gracious. 'Well, that settles everything, does it not? Of course I shall not pay you the salary which Miss Smithers enjoys. Let me see . . .'

She named a sum which, from the look of disgust on Miss Smithers's face, was well below the normal rate, but Jane answered quietly, 'Thank you, Lady Grimstone.' It might not be much but she would be able to save a good deal of it in a month; to be able to step straight into a job at the end of that time might not be possible and there were the animals.

In the car the professor said, 'I hope you are prepared for a rather disagreeable month . . .'

'Yes, I am, and thank you very much for helping me, Professor, I'm very grateful . . .'

'Save your gratitude.' He sounded mocking. 'I told you what kind of a job it would be.'

'I know that, but at least we can all have a home while I look around for a permanent job.'

He said casually, 'True enough. Be ready for me in the morning. Have you a great deal of luggage?'

'Two cases and the cats and Bruno. The girl who took over my flat when I came home has stored most of my things. Must I tell Basil?'

'Certainly not. He told you to leave and you are doing so; that should suffice. What about that nice woman—Bessy? Is she to go too?'

'He said she was to stay until he came but she won't do that. She has a sister in London—she wants to go there. She had to go to Blandford this morning to see the solicitor and arrange her annuity.'

'If she can be ready I'll take her to Blandford as we go.'

'You're very kind...'

'Dismiss the thought that I am a second Sir Galahad, I merely like to arrange matters in a satisfactory manner.'

Which speech so dampened Jane's spirits that she fell silent. At the house she asked diffidently if he cared to come in.

'Five minutes—I'll talk to Bessy.'

'She may not be back unless she got a lift. The bus doesn't leave until after lunch...' She stopped talking for she could see that he wasn't listening; indeed, he looked bored. She led him wordlessly to the drawing-room and went to see if Bessy had returned.

She had. Jane could hear her singing, slightly off key, in the kitchen. She looked up from peeling potatoes as Jane went in. 'Everything's settled, Miss Jane. That nice old man, 'e 'as everything just so, I put me name ter a paper or two and that's that. Money every month—what do you think of that, eh?'

'Wonderful, Bessy. Look, come quickly, will you? There's no time to tell you now, but I've got a job and am leaving tomorrow—the professor says if you want to go too he'll give you and your luggage a lift when he comes for me.'

Bessy was already taking off her pinny. 'It's a bit sudden, like, but I can't get away quick enough.' She trotted back with Jane and found the professor leaning out of an open window, looking at the view.

He explained quickly and very clearly so that Bessy took it all in without a lot of interrupting. 'I'll be ready and waiting, sir,' she said without any hesitation, 'and thank yer kindly. Me and Miss Jane, we can't get away from 'ere fast enough now Mrs Wesley's gone.'

'Good. I'll see you both tomorrow.'

'Will you have some lunch?' asked Jane, and went pink when he said gravely, 'I have no time, but thanks for the coffee I had earlier.'

She saw him to the door and watched him get into his car and drive away. There had been no need to remind her that she had made a fool of herself weeping all over him. He had been kind and helpful and indeed given her the chance to get away just when she was in despair. All the same, she wasn't sure if she liked him.

She had no time to waste thinking about him. She and Bessy had a sketchy meal in the kitchen and went about the business of packing. The house was already cleaned and polished; Basil would be unable to find fault with the way in which they had left it. Bessy telephoned her sister, cleaned out the fridge and, having packed her things, set about cooking a splendid meal for them both. As for Jane, she went down to the village and told the post office that they were leaving and could their letters be redirected, then she stopped the milk and warned the baker.

Mrs Bristow leaned over the counter. 'Is that Mr Basil coming to live here?' she wanted to know, and when Jane said that yes, he was, Mrs Bristow nodded. 'Well, love, you just go and enjoy yourself, you've earned it, I dare swear, you and Bessy both. Good luck to you. Not but what we shall all miss you.'

There wouldn't be much time in the morning; Jane went round the old house, bidding it a silent goodbye and shutting the windows and locking the doors. Basil had demanded a set of keys on his last visit and now she left her bunch of keys on their ring on the hall table and went along to the kitchen to eat her supper. They washed up together before she took Bruno and the cats for their last walk, and then, quite tired from their busy day, they went to their beds.

At breakfast Bessy said suddenly, 'I can't believe it, Miss Jane. After all these years, and you—it's been yer 'ome for most of yer life.'

'But it wouldn't be home if we stayed, Bessy, dear.'

'I'll 'ear from you?'

'Of course, Bessy, and I'll come and see you as soon as I can—before I go to a job. I shall try for something away from London but I promise you I'll come and see you first.'

She left Bessy to wash the few dishes and went in search of the animals, enjoying the morning sunshine in the garden; she had been careful not to let them see their baskets but all the same they were aware that something unusual was afoot; it would be most unfortunate if one of them decided to disappear just as the professor arrived. It was a relief when the small worry was resolved by a sudden chilly shower so that they trooped indoors where they settled in front of the fireless grate.

The professor was punctual and Jane lost no time in popping Percy and Simpkin into their baskets and fastening the lead on to Bruno's collar. By the time he had been admitted and was carrying out the cases, she was ready, composed in a tweed suit and sensible shoes, her glorious hair very neat, her lovely face hardly needing the powder and lipstick which she had discreetly applied.

The professor wasted no time in idle chat; his good-morning was brisk and beyond a matter-of-fact question as to whether the gas and electricity had been turned off and the windows and doors closed he saved his breath, stowed the animals in the back with Bessy, held the door for Jane to get in beside him and without a backward glance drove away. Jane, who had been dreading the last few minutes when they left, was thankful for the abruptness of their departure, but she couldn't resist a last look over her shoulder as they turned into the lane, suddenly annoyed with him because he had hurried them away; it would have been nice to have had a last quick walk through her home, a last stroll in the garden.

Without looking at her he said quietly, 'This is the best way, you know. Lingering goodbyes are much better avoided.' He was suddenly brisk. 'We'll take Bessy to the train first and see her on to it—there's time enough for that.'

At the last moment Bessy broke down. The professor had bought her ticket for her, put her cases on the train and stood with Jane on the platform. There were still a couple of minutes before the train was due to leave and Bessy appeared at the door, leaning out precariously. 'Oh, Miss Jane, you will write? I'll miss the 'ouse and you and the animals. Wasn't there no other way?'

Jane went and took her hand. 'Bessy, dear, it'll be all right, I promise you. Look, if I get a good job and can find somewhere to live, if you're not quite settled with your sister you can come and live with me then we'll be all together again.'

'Promise?'

'I promise, Bessy. I'll write to you in a day or two—we still have each other and I'm sure Granny would have approved of what we're doing.'

'That nasty old Basil.' Bessy wiped her eyes and managed a small smile and a moment later the train pulled out of the station. Jane waved until Bessy was nothing but a blur in the distance and then walked out of the station beside the professor. She wanted to have a good cry herself but that would have to wait.

She was distracted from her unhappy thoughts by the anxious mutterings and growls from the back of the car. The professor waited patiently while she soothed the animals, his face inscrutable, but she had no doubt that he was anxious to hand her over and be on his way. He had been kind in an impersonal way and after all, she reflected, he had got his own way, hadn't he? She had saved him the bother of finding someone to take Miss Smithers's place. All the same, she didn't like to try his patience too far.

She was surprised when he stopped outside an inn a mile or so out of the town. 'Coffee?' he suggested. 'I doubt if you will get it once you get to Lady Grimstone's.'

'Is there time?'

'Ample. I dare say Bruno would like to stretch his legs too.'

They didn't stay long but the coffee was hot and well made and the pub's bar cheerful and warm. Back in the car she asked diffidently, 'Have we upset your day? I do hope not. We—Bessy and I—are very grateful.'

'I did tell you that I had another visit to pay close by, did I not?'

He spoke coldly, so that she observed with a snap, 'Indeed you did, but one likes to express one's gratitude.'

'I stand corrected.' He spoke carelessly and with impatience. Really, she thought, he had done so much for them and she should like him enormously for that but now she wasn't sure if she liked him at all. But it was hard not to when they arrived, to find a decidedly bad-tempered Lady Grimstone waiting for them in the drawing-room.

'I expected you sooner than this, Miss Fox,' she snapped without bothering with a greeting.

'My fault,' said Professor van der Vollenhove. 'I was detained and had no way of letting Miss Fox know that I would be later than we had arranged.' He added blandly, 'Indeed, I am very sorry to have caused you and her so much worry.'

Lady Grimstone's high colour paled to a more normal shade. 'Oh, well, I must forgive you, I suppose. Will you stay for lunch? I should like to hear how your dear mother is—we have had so little time to talk.'

'I have an appointment in half an hour's time in Salisbury, much as I should have enjoyed staying. I shall be coming this way again in the near future;

perhaps you will invite me then. I must tell my mother how well you are looking.'

'I should so like to see her again.' Her eye lighted on Jane, standing quietly by the door. 'You can go, Miss Fox, find Miss Smithers—I expect you to take over from her without any inconvenience to myself.'

'Very well, Lady Grimstone.' Jane made her voice colourless. 'Goodbye, Professor van der Vollenhove.'

He went to open the door for her but he didn't say anything. Why should he? she thought dispiritedly; his plans had worked out very well and he could forget her. She went downstairs and found Miss Smithers waiting for her. 'I've put the cats and your dog in my room. Come and see them.'

'What about yours?'

'They're in the kitchen. I hope you don't mind but I'm going this afternoon—a friend with a car is coming to fetch me—it's too good a chance to miss.' She opened the door into her room. 'I've shut the outer door so they'll be quite safe here. There's everything they need in the conservatory and I thought it might be a good idea if I fetched Bill and we went into the garden together with the two dogs.'

'You're going today?' Jane suppressed panic. 'I haven't the least idea what to do...'

'Not to worry, I've written everything down for you. The staff will help you—they've been here for years— Lady Grimstone is no fun to work for but they're used to her and she pays them well.'

They released Percy and Simpkin, who began to prowl cautiously while Bruno sat watching them.

'Has Professor van der Vollenhove gone?' asked Miss Smithers.

'He was still in the drawing-room but he said that he had to go almost at once.'

'I'll get Bill from the kitchen and we'll have a quick run in the garden before Lady Grimstone rings. There's food for the cats already put out. I'll let you out of the garden door and meet you outside.'

Bill was elderly, good-natured and slow-moving; he stood patiently while Bruno circled him and decided to be friends and then wandered away in a ponderous fashion while Bruno made rings round him, pleased with his new friend.

'Oh, good, you'll not have any trouble with them, and I don't see why the cats shouldn't settle down too. When she rings I'll tell Lady Grimstone that you're unpacking—that will give you time to read through the notes I've written for you.' Miss Smithers smiled kindly. 'I'm sure you'll do and bless you for coming—this job suits me—not many people will accept pets—but I really need a break. I'm off to Scotland to my married sister.'

'I hope you have a lovely holiday—you'll let me know when you'll be back? If I get a job I'll need to give the date when I'll be free ...'

'I'll let you know in good time. If everything goes to plan it should be in four weeks' time.' She whistled to Bill and went away with him and Jane followed her presently, to sit down on the one easy-chair in the room and study Miss Smithers's instructions. They were concise and she would have been an idiot not to understand them; life, she could see, was going to be busy for the next four weeks—there was no menial work involved but any number of small chores: letter-writing, reading aloud, making conversation, accompanying Lady Grimstone if and when she chose to go out, walking Bill, making sure that she was settled each night and getting up in the small hours if Lady Grimstone chose to send for her—and at the bottom of the list Miss Smithers had written in her neat hand, 'Sorting wool, unpicking embroidery, unpicking knitting, finding specs, acting as go-between with various local charities. A half-day a week free but you will need to remind her.' This last sentence cheered her up; she could find out about buses to Blandford or Salisbury and if the buses didn't fit with her off-duty the village shop would see to her small wants.

Four weeks wasn't long, she told herself, making sure that she looked as much like a companion as possible. The bell went then and she went back upstairs and presented herself to Lady Grimstone.

Miss Smithers was there too, sitting quietly saying nothing while her employer reiterated Jane's duties and then ordered Jane to ring the bell. 'Since Miss Smithers is going on holiday I think we might drink to that,' and when a boot-faced elderly man came into the room she said, 'Blake, fetch the sherry—we wish to toast Miss Smithers, who is in the happy position of going on holiday.' Lady Grimstone fixed a beady eye on Jane. 'I only wish that my health allowed me to indulge in such extravagance.'

Miss Smithers said nothing; probably she had heard it all before, reflected Jane. 'I think that one is entitled to a holiday if one works hard for one's living.'

Lady Grimstone's complexion took on a dangerous hue. 'I'm sure you are entitled to your opinion, Miss Fox; you are, of course, talking of menial workers. Smithers has a pleasant, easy life here, as no doubt you will discover for yourself while she is away.'

They drank their thimblefuls of sherry and went downstairs to the dining-room, which was exactly as Jane had expected it to be—heavy with red chenille curtains and massive furniture, the table set with great elegance. She wondered why someone had gone to all that trouble when they were served a soup so thin that it might have been, and probably was, an Oxo cube dissolved in a pint of water, followed by very small lamb chops, each lost with its sprig of parsley on the splendid porcelain plate and accompanied by a side-plate on which were arranged very prettily one small potato, a sliver of carrot and a morsel of broccoli. Jane, who had a splendid appetite and pleasantly Junoesque proportions to sustain, made hers last as long as possible and hoped for a substantial pudding.

Blancmange—something she hadn't eaten and had hated since early childhood. She rose from the table still hungry, and resolved to stock up with biscuits as soon as she could get to the village shop.

Lady Grimstone, leading the way majestically from the dining-room, said over her shoulder, 'Miss Smithers, let us say *au revoir* now. Miss Fox, you are free until four o'clock after you have settled me for my nap. You will take Bill for a walk and take any telephone calls and open the afternoon post which you will bring with you at precisely the hour.'

She bade Miss Smithers goodbye and ascended the staircase with Jane on her heels. Lady Grimstone took her nap in the drawing-room, lying on a *chaise-longue* before a splendid fire, but before she could compose herself there was ten minutes' hard work for Jane. A shawl to be wrapped just so around the lady's well covered shoulders, a fine rug to be spread over the rest of her person, a small table fetched and a glass

of water, smelling salts, a fan and a clean handkerchief with a small bottle of lavender water arranged
upon it—and not anyhow; each item had its ap-
pointed place. Jane, finished at last to her employer's
satisfaction, thought that she looked like someone in
a Regency novel.

'You may now go and enjoy your afternoon,' said
Lady Grimstone graciously.

It would be a short afternoon, reflected Jane, it was
already two o'clock and Bill had to have his walk;
and how was she to answer the phone if she was
walking him? She didn't ask; time was too precious.

She found Miss Smithers in her room. 'I forgot to
tell you that Lady Grimstone doesn't like big meals.
There's a tin of digestive biscuits in the top drawer of
the dressing-table, you can stock up on your half-
day—you don't have to be in until ten o'clock and
there's a quiet little pub in the village where you can
get a good meal. Just tell them you're taking over
from me for a week or two and they'll look after you.
If you wanted to go to Blandford or Salisbury I'm
afraid you can't—the buses don't fit and, even if they
did, by the time you got there it would be time to
come back.' She smiled. 'It's only for a month and
the village shop has all the basics, newspapers and
magazines and so on. The postman, Ted, will take
your letters and bring anything you may want. You'll
be all right?'

A bit late to ask, thought Jane, and said that yes,
everything was fine. 'Then I'm off; the car's outside
for me. I've put the cats in.'

They shook hands and Miss Smithers went away
and presently Jane heard the car as it was driven away.

It was a clear chilly afternoon and she went along to the kitchen and collected Bill, exchanged the time of day with Mrs Gibb the cook and Petts, the grim-faced woman who had let them in. There was another woman there too, small and round. 'Sarah,' said Mrs Gibb, 'gives a hand round the house—comes each day.' She smiled at Jane. 'New to this kind of job, are you? Thought so—well, we'll all give you a helping hand if you need it.'

Jane thanked her, collected Bill and went back to her room, opened the door and let out Percy and Simpkin, also Bruno, and set off to explore the grounds. The garden around the house gave way presently to a shrubbery and a wide expanse of grass planted with ornamental trees and circled and criss-crossed by narrow paths—ideal for the animals since there was a twelve-foot wall surrounding them. She walked briskly, feeling the first chill of autumn, and as she walked she made plans. She would get the postman to take a note to the post office in the village; once she could get one of the nursing magazines delivered she could start to apply for a job. It might have to be temporary again but she had to have somewhere to go when she left Lady Grimstone, somewhere where the dog and cats would be welcome; she had better order the *Lady* too; failing a nursing post she could go as a companion at least for the time being while she found exactly what she wanted. She might have to go back to London...

She took her companions indoors, unpacked and then explored her room. It was comfortable enough and had its own small bathroom as well as the con-servatory. She had been lucky to get the job, she re-flected, a thought which led naturally enough to

Professor van der Vollenhove. Did he work in London, she wondered, or did he live in Holland and travel around? Probably the latter, she thought, if he was sufficiently well known. During her years in hospital she had met several medical men who travelled widely, famous not only in their own country but in half the world as well. Her thoughts lingered on him and she wondered if she would see him again. It seemed unlikely. She was puzzling over her feeling of regret at the thought when she glanced at her watch; time to see if there was any post and tidy herself ready for what she hoped would be tea and cake.

Bill had stayed in her room, perfectly happy with his new friends, and, not sure if Lady Grimstone wanted him or not, she left him there and went along to the kitchen. Mrs Gibbs was at the table, cutting wafer-thin bread and butter.

'The post?' asked Jane. 'I was told to collect it— do I come here for it?'

'The hall, miss, on the table under the tiger head. If you want to see the postman he's here every morning at half-past seven, having a cuppa with us. He'll take your letters and bring you anything from the shop. Been doing it for years for Miss Smithers.'

She glanced at the old-fashioned clock on the wall. 'Tea in ten minutes, miss; time you got that post and had it ready for her ladyship.'

Jane thanked her and fetched the few letters on the tray. She slit the envelopes and carried them upstairs just as the long case clock in the hall chimed the hour.

She went into the drawing-room quietly and paused. Lady Grimstone was snoring with tremendous gusto but Jane supposed that she wouldn't want the servants to see her like that, lying anyhow, when they brought the tea-tray. She opened the curtains and let in the early dusk and her employer woke with a snort and sat up.

'I must have dozed off after lunch—it was rather a heavy meal.' A remark Jane felt unable to answer as she unwound the shawl and rug and helped Lady Grimstone to her feet, eased her into her chair and handed the post. Just in nice time; the tea-tray, borne by Blake, arrived then—Earl Grey tea, milkless of course, bread and butter she could see through and very small fairy cakes. Lady Grimstone ate all but one of the cakes.

In bed at last, Jane reflected on her day. It hadn't been too bad; although dinner, for which she had been told to dress, had been as meagre as lunch and she had eaten half the biscuits as she got ready for bed and was still hungry; the roast pigeon and straw potatoes followed by semolina shape had done little to fill her. 'But it's only for a month,' she told Percy and Simpkin, curled up at the end of the bed, and Bruno from his basket growled gently. 'At least we're all together, thanks to Professor van der Vollenhove.' She fell asleep thinking about him.

CHAPTER THREE

By THE end of the third day Jane realised that the professor had been quite right: Lady Grimstone was an extremely difficult woman with whom to live. She was self-centred, selfish and quite uncaring about anything or anyone other than herself, although Jane had to admit that she had a fondness for animals. She suffered from a variety of complaints, all of them imaginary except for mild emphesema as far as Jane could make out, and she was forever trying out new diets, none of them, unfortunately for those who lived with her, of a substantial kind.

Jane ate all the biscuits which Miss Smithers had left for her and longed for her half-day so that she could replenish the tin. No wonder the professor hadn't stayed for lunch, she thought sourly; his vast frame needed a good deal more nourishment than a single lamb chop. He might have warned her—but there again, why should he, seeing that she had taken the job with her eyes open and she a grown woman, able to look after herself?

If life wasn't exactly rosy for herself, at least Bruno, Percy and Simpkin were happy and safe and Bill had become their devoted friend.

The postman had brought her a copy of the *Nursing Times* and last week's *Lady*. There hadn't been anything suitable in the *Lady* but she had answered two advertisements for ward sister posts, one in London and one in Manchester, and she had written out an advertisement, stressing the need for a living-out post because of the animals, offering to go anywhere in England. The postman had taken it with him and all she had to do was wait in patience.

Lady Grimstone had few visitors and depended upon Jane for company for a good deal of the day, keeping her busy with a dozen small chores, and talking endlessly about her youth. Jane wished that she would talk about the professor and his family but he was never mentioned; Lady Grimstone preferred to give details of the more exalted members of her family and Jane put on a listening face and murmured suitably while she pondered her future.

It was obvious by the end of the week that her employer wasn't going to do anything about her half-day unless she brought the matter up.

'Is it already a week since you came, Miss Fox?' Lady Grimstone sounded disbelieving. 'Well, I suppose you must have it since you expect it. I should have thought that you would have been quite content here, living as you do in such delightful surroundings.'

'I am very content,' Jane pointed out politely, 'but I do need to buy one or two things—toothpaste and stamps, and Percy and Simpkin do like those little crunchy biscuits...'

'Well, in that case, you had better have Saturday afternoon after you have settled me for my nap and taken Bill for his walk. I expect you back by ten o'clock at the latest, Miss Fox. Miss Smithers is never late.'

'I'm sure I shall be back before then,' said Jane; indeed, what was there to keep her out after she had had a meal at the pub Miss Smithers had recommended?

She bent her lovely head over a tangle of knitting Lady Grimstone had ordered her to put to rights, already planning a busy Saturday afternoon so that not a minute of it should be wasted.

Jane told herself that Lady Grimstone wasn't being deliberately slow in settling down for her afternoon nap on Saturday; certainly she took twice as long as usual, calling Jane back twice before she could at last escape, to give Bill one of the briskest walks he had ever had, take him back to the kitchen where Blake, who was disposed to be friendly even if very much on his dignity, had promised to keep an eye on him, see to her own three, and then, very neat in the tweed suit, walk to the village.

It was a chilly day but it was wonderful to be free even for such a short time and the village store was better than she had hoped for. She bought stamps and notepaper, the newest *Nursing Times* and *Lady*, the local weekly paper and a couple of paperbacks, and then she turned her attention to the biscuits.

The friendly soul behind the counter, with no one else in the shop, was disposed to chat. 'Miss Smithers she likes digestive, says they fill her up nicely, but rich tea's tasty. She always took a jar of Bovril too, said the water from the tap was hot enough to make a bedtime drink.'

So Jane bought two lots of biscuits and the Bovril as well and chose a few apples too; Lady Grimstone was, for the time being at least, allergic to fruit, so her household were forced to be allergic too until such time as she discovered a new diet...

Jane left her purchases in the shop, promising to collect them before five o'clock, and, advised by the good lady there, took the road out of the village towards Tarrant Hinton. A mile along it, she was assured, there was a cottage where tea was to be had.

The road was narrow and there was no traffic; Jane promised herself that next week she would take Bruno; he wasn't over-keen on long walks but he would be company.

The cottage, when she reached it, looked welcoming, its windows already lighted and a couple of cars parked outside. She went inside, into a small room, crammed with tables, made cheerful by a bright fire and old-fashioned wallpaper. The tea, when it came, was, she was delighted to see, old-fashioned too: scones and jam and cream, fresh fruit cake and a plate of buttered buns, accompanying a pot of tea large enough for two. She enjoyed every mouthful, exchanging cheerful remarks with other customers there and then, mindful of the time, she walked back in the gathering dusk to the shop, collected her purchases and, still with half an hour to spare before the inn opened, went to inspect the church.

It was a beautiful building, thirteenth-century, its slender spire over a hundred feet high, and it was as beautiful inside as it was out, dim, faintly damp and very quiet, freshly arranged flowers softening the greyness of the stone. She stayed for a little while, soothed and comforted, her troubled future no longer menacing her so that she crossed the street presently feeling almost happy and certainly more hopeful.

She went through the open door of the inn rather hesitantly but was put at her ease at once by the stout man behind the bar.

'Evenin'—you'm be the young lady giving our Miss Smithers an 'and—glad to see you. You'll be wanting a bit of supper, no doubt.'

The bit of supper was steak and kidney pie, a pile of feather-light mashed potatoes and cabbage cooked with a dash of nutmeg and plenty of butter. There was apple pie and cream for pudding and a thick cup of coffee to finish. Jane lingered over her supper, reflecting how strange it was that a good meal and a change of scene could make the world of difference, and the inn was a pleasant place. She sat talking long after she had finished her meal but no one there showed any curiosity about her; they talked about Miss Smithers, whom they all liked, avoided speaking of Lady Grimstone and gave a variety of opinions about what sort of winter they would have—nice, undemanding talk. She got to her feet reluctantly at last and was surprised when a lad of sixteen or so joined her.

'Miss Smithers—she were nervous after dark,' he said in a mumbling voice, 'so me dad told me to see her home, so I'll do the same for you likewise.'

Jane paused at the door. 'There's really no need...'

But the innkeeper called across. 'Just you let young Ron walk with you, miss. It's dark and you've no torch—happen you'll get lost, solitary-like.'

So she left followed by a chorus of friendly 'goodnights' and had to admit to herself that she was glad of Ron's company. There was a moon, sliding in and out of the clouds, but there was a cold wind now, rustling through the high hedges and trees. Not a nervous girl, she was quite pleased to have someone with her. Once started on their walk, Ron lost his shyness; he was, he told her proudly, going to own a farm when he was old enough. 'I works for Farmer Morrish over Tarrant Gunville way, learning me way, as it were. 'E says I got a way with pigs...'

'Do tell me all about it,' urged Jane. It passed the time nicely and when they reached the gates of Lady Grimstone's house she had acquired a flow of information about sows, boars and piglets, not to mention the advantages of a saddleback over a large white.

'Miss Smithers, she'm interested in pigs, too,' volunteered Ron as they said goodnight. ''Appen you'll be coming next week, miss?'

'Oh, I do hope so,' said Jane. She had really enjoyed her few hours of freedom.

Blake admitted her with the observation that Lady Grimstone wished her to go to the drawing-room upon her return. She went to her room, deposited her parcels, reassured the three animals and then went back upstairs.

'You have returned,' observed Lady Grimstone—the statement seemed unnecessary. 'I trust you have had an enjoyable day...'

'Half-day, Lady Grimstone,' Jane reminded her politely. 'You wish to see me?'

'No, no! Merely to know that you had returned.'

'Then goodnight, Lady Grimstone,' said Jane. She glanced at the clock and saw that there was still a good half-hour before her half-day was officially over.

Her employer, no fool, said crossly, 'I shall not need you again until the morning, Miss Fox. Goodnight.'

There were replies to her applications for jobs on Monday morning; although her qualifications were satisfactory they were unanimous in their refusal to accept animals. As soon as she had a moment to spare she wrote off to several more hospitals as well as three jobs offered in the *Lady*. There was still plenty of time, she assured herself, and in the meantime she and Bruno, Percy and Simpkin were living in comfort.

She had had the cheque for five hundred pounds too, which gave her a false feeling of security. True, Lady Grimstone was a hard taskmistress and despite the biscuits she was often hungry, for the lady had now discovered a diet which precluded any kind of fat and since the diet went hand in glove with brisk exercise she had taken to getting up for her breakfast and eating it with Jane—special cereal like shredded cardboard, dry toast spread with a vegetable extract and coffee taken with skimmed milk. Despite the biscuits Jane was losing weight.

She had several answers on Saturday morning but she had no chance to read them until, with Bruno on his lead, she set off for the village and her few hours of freedom. It had turned wintry but she found a tree stump on the verge of the lane and sat down to read her letters. All her applications had been refused; despite her thick winter jacket and leather boots she suddenly felt cold. There were only two weeks left . . .

She walked on and, since there was no one else to talk to, talked to Bruno. 'It'll be all right,' she assured him. 'We've enough money to live on for a month or so and that's a long time.' It would have to be somewhere not too far away, certainly not London but not too close to Basil.

She collected her magazines, did her shopping and went along to the cottage to have her tea, to walk back presently with Bruno, collect her shopping and cross over to the inn.

They welcomed her as an old acquaintance, gave Bruno a bowl of water and a bone which he took under the table and enjoyed while she ate her supper— cottage pie, parsnips and potatoes in their jackets and jam roly-poly to follow. While she ate she joined in

the cheerful talk to-ing and fro-ing in the bar and afterwards young Ron walked her back, this time en-
lightening her as to the rearing of free-range chickens.

There were several likely jobs going when she
searched her magazines and she applied for them all
and waited hopefully, putting up with Lady
Grimstone's ill humour, due, she felt sure, to the
dreary diet. The days had turned crisp and Bill was
reluctant to go out for more than ten minutes at a
time although he was happy to sit in the conservatory
with her own animals, but on the following Saturday
morning the sun shone and there was no frost. Bidden
to walk with Bill, Jane took them all out into the
grounds, the cats walking sedately by her and the two
dogs foraging happily among the shrubbery. The small
respite from the particularly difficult unravelling of
Lady Grimstone's tapestry work gave her a chance to
read her letters. Quite a batch; she opened them one
by one and then stuffed them in her pocket, disappointed. She had a week left; she would take paper
and envelopes with her to the village that afternoon
and answer every single advertisement which offered
a possible job. Not necessarily nursing—a domestic
job where there would be no objection to her pets and
a free roof over her head, and if she heard nothing
before she left Lady Grimstone she would go to
Blandford and stay at one of the small bed and
breakfast places. She could of course ask Mr
Chepstow for help, but he might, in mistaken
kindness, tell Basil... She became aware that the dogs
were barking excitedly and turned to see what had
excited them.

Professor van der Vollenhove was only a yard or
two behind her and since they were well into the

shrubbery by now he was screened from the house, walking steadily towards her, elegant and unhurried and unsmiling.

She was surprised at the rush of pleasure she felt at the sight of him but her, 'Good afternoon, Professor,' was cool.

'You didn't expect me?' he asked, not bothering to greet her.

'No. Should I have done?'

'Common decency dictates that I should at least find out how you are getting on.'

'How kind——' her eyes flashed greenly '—but you have no need to concern yourself about me.'

'Oh, I am not concerned.' He was annoyingly casual. 'Just curious. Is this your free time?'

'No, no. Just taking Bill for his walk, I'm free...' She stopped and bit her lip and he said easily,

'This afternoon. Good, I feel like a good walk; we can take Bruno and have a meal somewhere.'

'You're very kind...' Why did she keep saying that like an idiot? 'I'm not sure if Lady Grimstone...'

'Leave her to me. You get on well with her?' He laughed suddenly. 'What an unfair question, I won't expect an answer. Let us go back to the house.'

They parted at the conservatory. 'I'll see you later,' was all he said and whistled to Bill to go with him.

She had barely tidied herself before the bell went and she went upstairs to find Lady Grimstone in her usual chair and the professor sitting by her.

'Go and tell Blake that Professor van der Vollenhove will be having lunch,' said Lady Grimstone, and Jane escaped thankfully and took so long about it that her employer said very sharply, 'What took you so long?' and shook her head im-

patiently because the professor had got to his feet
when Jane went back into the room. The girl was far
too pretty.

Jane took no part in the conversation at lunch
although the professor directed several remarks to her
while they ate their way through shredded carrots and
celery, very small portions of grilled sole and yoghurt
to follow. Jane, as usual, got up from the table as
hungry as when she had sat down and she had no
doubt that the professor felt the same. Serve him right
for poking his nose in, she reflected peevishly.

'Such a pleasure seeing you again, Nikolaas,' declared Lady Grimstone. 'I'm tempted to forgo my
afternoon rest—so essential to me in my poor state
of health—so that you can tell me more news of your
mother.'

She glanced at Jane. 'You can go, Miss Fox. I'm
sure you won't mind remaining here for an hour or
so; I'll call you when the professor goes so that you
can make me comfortable before you go out.'

Hot protest almost scalded Jane's tongue but,
before she could put it into words, Professor van der
Vollenhove spoke.

'That would have been delightful but unfortunately
I have an engagement and must tear myself away. I
shall be coming this way in a week's time—may I call
and see you then?'

'Of course, dear boy,' Lady Grimstone was all
graciousness, 'come to lunch; you know that you are
always very welcome.' She looked at Jane. 'You can
go, Miss Fox; give Bill his run and come back here
in ten minutes.'

Jane said, 'Yes, Lady Grimstone,' and in the same colourless voice, 'Goodbye, Professor van der Vollenhove.'

He opened the door for her and she went past him without looking at him. If she could have trodden on his feet she would have done so.

When she went back her employer was alone and disposed to be chatty while Jane heaved her on to the sofa and began the tedious business of arranging shawls and scarves just so and cluttering up the little side-table with all the unnecessary bits and pieces essential for the lady's nap.

'A delightful man,' observed Lady Grimstone and added, 'and so clever. Well known—of course—famous in the medical field. Wealthy too... He will of course marry suitably.'

Jane had nothing to say to this. She didn't care tuppence about the professor, only let him keep his arrogant nose out of her business. She was aware that the thought was ungrateful; he had come to her aid just when she needed it most but then he had had no need to put himself out to do that, had he?

She went to her room finally, saw to Percy and Simpkin, got into her coat, tied a scarf over her brilliant hair and fastened Bruno's lead. A good brisk walk in the fresh air would improve her temper.

She was a hundred yards from the gate when the Bentley crept up beside her. The professor opened the door. 'Get in,' he invited without as much as a please so that she felt constrained to say at once,

'No, I won't—I'm going for a walk.'

'Splendid; we'll park the car by the inn and go back there for tea.'

She said coolly, 'No, thank you. Besides, Bruno is with me.'

He said in his placid voice, 'We're wasting time. Do get in, Jane—and Bruno, too, of course.'

'Why?'

'I have had no opportunity of asking you how you are getting on here.'

It *would* be nice to talk to someone—she got in, still a little cross, and Bruno settled down at her feet.

They didn't speak during the brief drive to the village. They stopped at the inn, parked the car and, at the professor's suggestion, Jane went to the shop, bought her magazines and biscuits and took them back to it. He came out of the inn as she reached the car. 'We can have tea here at half-past four if that suits you.'

He didn't wait for her to answer but walked her off at a brisk pace, away from the village street until they came to a bridle path.

'This will take us to the Roman road; we can cut back through Hog's Bottom and join the lane past the church.'

She was surprised. 'You know this part of the country?'

'I came here several times with my parents and when I was at Oxford I came occasionally for weekends.'

'Oh, I see.' She stopped to let Bruno run free. For something to say she added, 'It's a pretty village and the people are nice too...'

'Yes. How are you getting on with Lady Grimstone?'

'Quite well, thank you.'

'She is a remarkably rude woman—she always has been and she is too old to mend her ways now. I dare say you have found your stay here trying.'

'Well, yes, but it has given me time to make some plans.'

'You go next Saturday?'

'I believe so, although we haven't heard from Miss Smithers yet—I'm to stay until she returns.'

'You have heard from Bessy?'

'Yes. I think she finds London rather different from the country but I expect she'll settle down.'

'And you, Jane?'

'I am perfectly content, thank you, Professor.'

'I'm to mind my own business, am I? In that case let us discuss the weather . . .'

'I'm very grateful——' began Jane.

'Spare me that, Jane. I don't wish for your gratitude. Tell me, are the servants helpful?'

She was relieved to talk about something else. 'Yes, very, and loyal to Lady Grimstone too.'

'They're well paid,' he told her drily.

They walked on in silence for some time with Bruno rushing to and fro on his short legs, uttering small barks of pleasure, and presently they took a cross-country path bordering a field of winter wheat and joined a narrow lane.

Jane had to admit to herself that she was enjoying her afternoon.

The professor began a rambling conversation which required only the most casual of replies; by the time they reached the village her usual good temper was restored and the idea of tea was welcome.

The inn was shut but they went round to the back and were ushered into a small room behind the bar and told to sit themselves down at the table. She had the impression that teas were not normally served and it was being done to oblige the professor.

It was young Ron who brought in the tray followed by his mother with a plate of hot buttered toast in one hand and a large jam sponge in the other. Ron set out the cups and saucers and the teapot just so and beamed at Jane.

'Shan't need to walk you back tonight, miss,' he said cheerfully. 'Reckon the professor here will be doing that.'

He grinned widely at them both and went away.

Professor van der Vollenhove ignored Jane's pink cheeks. 'I certainly shan't walk you back—I've booked a table at Plumber Manor and I rely on the car to get us back here.'

She fastened on the one important fact. 'You're not staying at Lady Grimstone's . . . ?'

He smiled a little at the misgiving in her voice. 'No, no. I shall be going back to town.' He offered her toast. 'You know Plumber Manor?'

'Oh, yes—I've been there once or twice. It's very kind of you to ask me but I'm not dressed for dining out . . .'

He ran an eye over her charming person, clad in silvery grey jersey. The dress was by no means the height of fashion but it had a timeless elegance.

'You need have no fear on that score; you appear to be quite suitably dressed.'

A non-committal remark which did nothing for her ego.

He began to talk about nothing in particular then so that by the time they had finished their tea she was talking to him quite happily about her work at the hospital and the people she had met.

It was cosy in the inn parlour; an hour went past pleasantly enough but presently the professor suggested that she might like to go and tidy herself. 'I booked a table for half-past seven—rather early but I do have to get back to town as you know and besides it would never do for us to get back to Lady Grimstone's too late—think of having to knock up Blake to let us in.'

He drove back to the Blandford road, took the fork at the brige and followed the narrow winding road to Sturminster Newton, a journey of less than half an hour. The evening was dark, windy and moonless and he made no attempt to hurry, so that it was after seven o'clock when they arrived.

The restaurant was in a Jacobean manor house, standing well back from the road in spacious grounds and a mile or two from Sturminster Newton. The dining-room was a charming room, tastefully furnished. They had drinks before going to their table and Jane, by now healthily hungry, read the menu with delight.

'I don't know about you, but I'm famished,' observed the professor. 'I do hope you are not one of those women who peck at their food and worry about their shapes.'

Jane went faintly pink. 'I'm quite a big sort of person,' she pointed out, 'and I do get hungry...'

'So I would imagine if lunch was anything to go by. What about the lobster mousse to start with?'

She agreed happily and chose noisettes of lamb with tarragon sauce, creamed potatoes and tiny sprouts, while the professor settled for a tournedos in red wine and contented himself after that with the cheese board. Jane, after deliberation, chose chocolate marquise . . .

She poured their coffee and looked at the time. 'How long will it take to drive back?'

He selected a *petit four* and gave it to Bruno, who was sitting silently under the table. 'Less than half an hour. Don't worry, I won't let you be late.' He took the coffee she offered him. 'You leave on Saturday—have you a job to go to?'

She stirred her coffee and didn't look at him. 'Oh, yes, yes, I have.'

'Jane . . .' She could hear the amusement and the disbelief in his voice.

She was no liar, she reflected crossly. 'Well, I have several answers to advertisements . . .'

'You have somewhere to go until you decide which one to accept?'

'I know London quite well; there won't be any trouble finding a room for a few days.'

'With your three animals?' His voice was gentle.

'Yes. With them.'

'Not good enough, Jane. I have friends who will be delighted to put you—all of you—up for as long as necessary. I'll come down on Saturday afternoon and collect you.'

She met his eyes across the table; he was smiling a little but he had spoken decisively and she suspected that he wasn't going to take no for an answer. Suddenly she realised that it wouldn't do at all. He had come into her life unexpectedly and she was going to have to let him go out of it again as quickly as possible. She hadn't been entirely certain how she felt about him until now—he had seemed a mixture of austere kindness and indifference and, now and again, a friend. But never mind all that now—she liked him; he interested her, she would like very much to know more about him, to see more of him, but that wouldn't do, she had her living to earn and the sooner she set about that the better. He had found her a welcome respite but that was all it was and she suspected that if she saw more of him she might get to like him rather more than she had bargained for.

She said, 'That's very kind of you but I wouldn't want to put your friends to any trouble.'

'Good, then that's settled. I should be at Lady Grimstone's around three o'clock. Now I think we must be going.'

She was rather silent on the way back but he appeared not to notice and when he stopped before the house he got out, opened her door and said pleasantly, 'You still have ten minutes; just time to let patient Bruno stretch his legs.'

He took her arm and walked her round the side of the house to the path leading to the shrubbery. A fitful moon was avoiding the clouds as best it could so that it wasn't completely dark although it was chilly enough.

'I enjoyed my evening,' said Jane, very conscious of his arm. 'Thank you very much.'

'My pleasure, Jane. When you write to Bessy please give her my regards.' He added carelessly, 'Whereabouts does she live now?'

'In Stepney, with a sister. I hope she will be happy there, the address is "The Cott, Greenfield", which come to think of it doesn't sound right for Stepney. I've had two or three letters from her and they're rather...sparse, but perhaps that's because she doesn't like writing. I said I'd go and see her before I start another job. I wouldn't like her to be unhappy; she spent almost all her working life looking after Granny.'

'A friend as well as a servant—the salt of the earth.' He turned her round and started back towards the house, whistling to Bruno as he did so. 'Have you a key?' and at her low chuckle, 'No, of course not, how silly of me to ask. Blake lets you in, but which door?'

'The side-door leading to the garden-room. His quarters are close by, you see, and it's convenient.'

He said nothing and it was too dark for her to see his frown.

At the door he rang the bell and she sensed his impatience as they waited for Blake to open it, and when he did the professor bade her goodnight and shook her hand, nodded to Blake and stood there until she was inside and the door bolted behind her.

''Ad a nice evening, miss?' asked Blake.

'Yes, thank you, Blake. Goodnight.' She went to her room, saw to the cats and Bruno and got herself to bed. She had enjoyed every minute of her half-day, and it was only on the point of sleep that she remembered that she wasn't going to see the professor again; job or no job, she would be gone by the time he came on Saturday. It was a mean trick on her part to let him think that she would go to his friends but on the spur of the moment she couldn't think of anything else to do, and good sense told her that to get involved with him was something not to be considered.

She puzzled over what to do all through Sunday, and on Monday she woke early, lying in bed, thinking what was best to be done and getting the beginnings of a headache. She ate her breakfast without much appetite, and saw to Percy and Simpkin, took Bruno

and Bill for their morning run and went indoors,
where she encountered Blake.

'Letters for you, miss.' He unbent sufficiently to
allow himself a faint smile as she took them. Three—
she had applied for five posts and had given up hope
of hearing from any of them. There were still ten
minutes before she needed to go to Lady Grimstone;
she hurried to her room and read the first of them.
A nice letter, but regretfully no animals were allowed.
The second would allow the cats but no dog; the third,
written in a spidery hand from Carlisle, would be glad
of her services as soon as possible. A private hospital,
the writer went on, caring for a number of patients.
Should she wish to bring her cats and dog, that could
be allowed, but she must realise that this was a concession only allowable since the need for a trained
nurse was paramount. The hospital stood in its own
grounds and she could live in a small cottage close by
the hospital building. The salary was a good deal less
than she was entitled to, but she would be on her own
and the animals would be safe. It was a long way to
go, too. Her heart failed her at the thought but only
for a moment. She had already sent the names of ref-
erees; all she had to do was to accept, subject to a
month's notice on either side.

Unmindful of Lady Grimstone's needs, she hastily
wrote accepting the post and took the letter to the
kitchen and asked one of the women who came from
the village each day to post it when she went home
at midday.

That done, she raced up to Lady Grimstone's room
to find that lady in a very nasty temper. 'A good thing
that you are leaving, Miss Fox,' she declared wrath-
fully. 'You are becoming extremely slack. I have a

letter from Miss Smithers this morning; she will be returning on Saturday morning and not before time. Arrange to leave as soon after her return as possible.'

Something which suited Jane's plans admirably.

After lunch, eaten in a disapproving silence, she settled her employer and took Bill and Bruno for their walk and this time, with them safely on their leads, she went to the phone box at the end of the lane outside the grounds and found out about trains. It wouldn't be an easy journey but she had been told to leave as soon as Miss Smithers returned; she would be well on her way once the professor arrived, and with luck she would arrive that same evening.

On Tuesday she got grudging permission to go to Blandford so that she might pay in her wages cheques and draw out what money she would need for her journey, and at the same time she got train tickets for herself and Bruno; the cats, she hoped, would be allowed to travel with her. It was by no means an ideal way of travelling and she dreaded it, more for their sakes than hers. However, she had unexpected help from the landlord of the inn, who, when she returned on the bus, told her that he would be going into Salisbury on Saturday morning and would gladly give her a lift, something which would save her a good deal of bother. She accepted gratefully and went back to her duties with a lighter heart.

There was another letter from Miss Smithers the next day, stating that she would be back soon after nine o'clock on Saturday morning since she intended to spend the night with friends in Blandford. Everything was going splendidly, Jane told herself, resolutely refusing to think about the professor.

The week went very slowly, or so it seemed to her. She packed on Friday, took care that the animals would be as comfortable as possible on the journey and was up betimes on Saturday morning. She was to be fetched at ten o'clock and, provided that she caught the train she intended, she would be in London by two o'clock at the latest and there was an afternoon train to Carlisle she hoped to catch. Everything, she assured herself, was going to be all right.

Strangely enough, it was. Miss Smithers arrived very punctually, Jane lost no time in bidding her employer, still annoyed with her, goodbye, and skipped into the pub landlord's van with the animals perched in the back, where she waved a final goodbye to Blake and his colleagues and Miss Smithers and was driven to Salisbury. It wasn't easy getting in and out of trains and queueing for a taxi in London but she caught her train and settled down for the long journey to the north. The open compartment was almost empty, the cats sat quietly in their baskets and Bruno crouched at her feet, and Jane sighed with relief and sat back, speculating on her new job. Her one regret was that she hadn't been able to see Bessy, although she had written explaining why she had broken her promise and telling her that as soon as she had a long weekend or holidays she would contrive to get back to London to see her; no easy undertaking, for she would have to put the animals in kennels while she was away; she began to worry about that and then, weary from the journey, dozed off.

CHAPTER FOUR

PROFESSOR VAN DER VOLLENHOVE arrived at Lady Grimstone's house shortly after three o'clock and on being admitted enquired after that lady and, hearing that she was still resting, asked that Miss Fox should be told that he had arrived.

'Miss Fox left this morning shortly before ten o'clock, sir,' said Blake, poker-faced.

If he had expected the professor to show surprise or annoyance he was to be disappointed. The professor's face remained impassive so that Blake continued, 'There's a letter for you, sir, and Miss Smithers I'm sure would be glad to see you—she returned today.'

Miss Smithers could have been waiting for her cue in the wings, for she opened a door and crossed the hall to shake hands with the professor, and when Blake had withdrawn said, 'Come to my room; you came to see Jane, of course?'

He didn't reply and as they sat down she said, 'She told me that she had found a job where the cats and dog would be welcome.'

'I'm glad—where is that?'

'I don't know—when I asked her she just said that it was a long way from here. The landlord of the pub might know; he left her at the station in Salisbury. You expected to find her here?'

'Yes. This job—probably too good an opportunity to miss . . .'

'Well, read her letter while I get Blake to bring us some tea. Lady Grimstone won't need me for another half an hour or so. You'll stay and see her?'

'Oh, yes, but only briefly—I must get back to town this evening.'

Alone, he opened Jane's letter. It was a stiff little note; he guessed that she had written it several times before she had been satisfied with it. She had had an unexpected job offered to her which seemed exactly what she wanted and she was sorry that he had not found her at Lady Grimstone's but there had been no chance to do more than write a note. She was his sincerely, Jane Fox.

He read the letter again slowly; it wasn't at all the kind of letter that he would have expected from her and there was no hint as to where she had gone. He sighed, knowing that against his better judgement he was going to have to find out.

He drank his tea presently while Miss Smithers dwelt on the delights of Scotland and, when Lady Grimstone's bell rang, accompanied her to the drawing-room where he spent an hour patiently listening to the old lady's grumbling voice.

'You were quite satisfied with Miss Fox?' he asked at length.

'Satisfied? My dear Nikolaas, she did her work well enough, I suppose, and Bill liked her, but she is so—so alive. All that bright red hair and her eyes—her voice would be so meek and they would flash green fire. A very unsettling young woman.'

He agreed silently but aloud he said, suitably grave, 'I'm sorry if I made a bad choice, but you have Miss Smithers back now.'

'Oh, I'm not ungrateful, Nikolaas; as I said, she did her work well enough.'

'She has another post, Miss Smithers tells me.'

'Has she? I didn't ask and she said nothing to me. She is the kind of girl who will always fall on her feet.' Lady Grimstone dismissed Jane with a toss of the head. 'Now, tell me about your mother. She is well?'

He stayed another half-hour and then took his leave, but before he went he sought out Miss Smithers. 'If you hear from Jane, will you let me know?' He tore a leaf from his pocket book. 'This number will always find me sooner or later.'

'Yes, of course I will, Professor.' Miss Smithers eyed him thoughtfully. 'Don't worry about her; she's twenty-seven, you know, and very capable.' She added, 'Do try the inn . . .'

He thanked her and got into the Bentley, drove to the village and went into the pub. Ron saw him first and came to meet him.

'Come ter see our miss? She's gone—Dad took 'er to Salisbury this morning.' He looked over his shoulder. 'Dad, 'ere's the professor come for Miss Jane.'

'Took 'er to Salisbury station this very morning; put 'er on the London train with them animals.'

The professor said casually, 'Ah, yes, she has an old family servant living in London.'

'Right you are there, sir, but she wasn't going to see 'er. Said she 'ad nice time to catch her train and I says ter 'er, ''and just you take a taxi with all that luggage and the cats and dog''. She said she would too.'

'Good of you to take her to the train,' the professor observed quietly. 'If she writes to you will you let Miss Smithers know? She forgot to get the address.'

'As good as done, sir, and 'ow about one on the 'ouse?'

'Tempting, but I'm driving back to London. I'll be down again of course.'

Father and son watched him drive away. ''E's just right for our Miss Jane,' observed young Ron.

'That's as maybe, but 'oo's ter know if they'll meet up again?'

It was well into the evening by the time Jane and her impediments got off the train at Carlisle. It had been an InterCity Express but even then the journey had seemed to go on forever, an opinion shared by her companions, who mewed gently at her from their baskets while Bruno, stout-hearted as always, looked hungry.

She was to take a taxi, the letter of acceptance had said; the hospital was just outside Carlisle, a matter of a mile or so. A good many people had got off the train and there was a queue for taxis but now she was almost at the end of her journey and nothing could depress her. When her turn finally came the cabby turned out to be a nice fatherly man who helped her with her case and cats, settled her and Bruno into their seats and wanted to know where she was going. When she told him he asked, 'A nurse, are you, miss? Short of staff there, I did hear. They'll be glad to see you. It's not far, a bit quiet like just outside the town. Know these parts?'

She hardly noticed where they were going as they chatted cheerfully but presently they turned off the road through a wide gate and drove up a gravelled drive and stopped before a red-brick building, austere and with its windows curtained over.

She got out, paid the cabby, who had taken her case to the door for her and waited until it was opened before calling a cheery goodbye, and, on being bidden to enter by a large friendly-looking woman, did so.

'You're to go straight to Matron,' she told Jane. 'Leave the little dog here; I'll stay till you come back and then show you where to go. Could you do with some supper?'

'Oh, yes, please.'

'It'll have to be in the kitchen—supper was over hours ago, but I'll find you something and the cats and dog too.'

'You're very kind.'

Matron was a small wiry woman with dark hair which should have been grey upon which was perched an elaborate muslin cap. Her uniform was navy blue and fitted her to perfection. Her eyes were brown, rather small and a little too close together. Jane told herself that first impressions were often wrong and wished her a polite good-evening.

'Sit down, Miss Fox. The housekeeper will show you where you are to live presently. I dare say you are tired after your journey. I hope that you appreciate the fact that you are allowed to have your pets with you. They are well behaved?'

'Yes, Matron.'

'We are at the moment rather short-staffed. We have over thirty patients—this as you know is a privately run hospital. There are twenty-two single rooms, five two-bedded rooms and one small ward of four beds. You will be in charge of the single rooms—night duty—as well as the ward and the doubles. They are all at the moment occupied. We have a different system from the NHS here—a fortnight on duty and four nights off. You will go on duty at half-past eight each evening and work until half-past eight in the morning. Your meal will be served at midnight and of course in a hospital such as this you will have plenty of leisure during the night.'

'How many nurses work with me?' asked Jane.

'Normally three, but one of my most senior nurses is away sick at the moment. You will find them willing girls and very few patients need much attention during the night. I suggest that you come on duty for an hour or so tomorrow at lunchtime and I will show you round; you will need a little time to settle in. Come here at ten tomorrow, please, Miss Fox. Goodnight.'

The housekeeper introduced herself as Miss Forbes. 'Nice little dog,' she observed. 'Now you come along with me. Leave your case, we'll take it over presently after supper.'

She led the way through the austere hall through a door at the back down a few steps and into a large kitchen, pleasantly warm but rather cluttered. 'Sit down, do. I'll give the little dog some water, shall I? And I dare say I can find him a biscuit or two.'

'You're very kind. I'll find them their supper as soon as I've had mine. I don't like to take the cats from their baskets until we're all together and the doors are shut.'

'Quite right too.' She came to the table with a bowl of soup and then cold beef and bread and butter. 'And a cup of tea to finish with? There is a shop close by but I can get the milkman to leave an extra pint for you if you like. The nurses buy their packets of tea and biscuits from me when they want them.'

'Then may I have them too, please? I'll take them with me if I may.'

The housekeeper went away and came back with teabags and biscuits and a small bag of sugar. 'What about the cats?'

'I've enough food for a day for them all...'

'Just you write down what you want and I'll put it on the grocer's list and you can pay me.'

'You're very kind.' Jane finished her supper, drank her tea and got up. 'I hope I haven't spoilt your evening. The supper was lovely.'

'You needed it,' said Miss Forbes. 'I'll take you to your place.'

They went out of a back door across a wide yard to the end of one wing of the building. Built on to it was a very small cottage, its back wall the wall of the hospital, its front facing what looked in the dark to be a kitchen garden. Miss Forbes produced a key and opened its small door. It led straight into a low-ceilinged room, sparsely furnished with a table, easy-chair, bookshelves and two straight-backed chairs. It was cold too. 'Bedroom's on t'other side,' said Miss Forbes and opened another door. The room was even smaller but the bed, freshly made up, looked comfortable and there was a very small shower-room leading from it. 'Kitchen tucked in behind.' The housekeeper pointed out a cupboard-like space partitioned off from the living-room. 'There's a gas fire, you put your own fifty-pence pieces in. Gas ring in the kitchen. Probably some gas left from Sister Bright...'

'Is that the one who's ill?'

'No. The one who left.' The housekeeper didn't say any more and Jane didn't like to ask. Miss Forbes tried the gas. 'You're in luck, there's enough to start you off. Got any money?'

Jane looked in her purse. 'Two fifty-pence pieces...'

'Put 'em both in now. Someone'll have change in the morning—try and keep four or five handy here. See you at breakfast—eight o'clock sharp. Come in through the kitchen and I'll show you where.'

They wished each other goodnight and Jane locked the door, pulled the faded curtains over the windows and let the cats out of their baskets.

First things first, she told them, and put on their harnesses, put Bruno on his lead and opened the door again, glad that she had a torch in her case. She locked the door behind her and led her charges across the rough grass before the cottage. There was a wall at the end of it, extending on either side of her for as far as she could see. In daylight she would be able to see more; for the moment the rough grass was quite adequate.

Back in the cottage she fed Percy and Simpkin, gave Bruno his supper and invited them to sit before the fire while she unpacked, undressed, showered with some difficulty and, in her dressing-gown, curled up beside them by the little fire. The three of them crept close after a few minutes, sensing that they might settle down to a quiet orderly way of life once more; it had been a nightmare of a day. 'Now everything will be all right,' Jane told them, and presently took herself off to bed in the tiny bedroom, to be joined by all three of them within minutes. They made rather a crowd but they were warm and comforting. Full of optimism, and allowing herself only the briefest of thoughts about the professor, she fell asleep.

It was still dark when the alarm clock woke her. She got up, lighted the fire and squeezed her splendid person into the cramped shower-room once more. She had no uniform but, according to the letter, she would be supplied with that, so she dressed, got into her coat and took the animals outside. It was a raw morning, struggling to take over from the wintry night, and just light enough now for her to get her bearings. The hospital wasn't large, with two upper floors and wings on either side, to the end of one of which Jane's cottage was attached. She had only a dim idea of the grounds in the front of the building but here at the back was a wide strip of rough grass with a wall beyond, presumably the kitchen garden. The grass, while uninteresting, provided a good stamping ground for the cats and Bruno; the cats, at least, had no desire to stay out of doors in the cold, and she could take Bruno for a good walk before she went to bed and again in the evening before she went on duty. Things could have been a great deal worse.

Mindful of Miss Forbes's instructions she went into the hospital by the back door and then, since she had no idea of where to go, to the kitchen. Miss Forbes wasn't there, but an untidy girl in a rough apron jerked her head over one shoulder. 'Upstairs, dining-room's on the left.'

It was hardly a staircase, four or five steps leading to a higher level which brought her out into the hall again. There were several doors but she could hear voices beyond a half-open door and went in.

The room was furnished with the minimum of pieces—a long table down its centre, half a dozen chairs on either side and a sideboard. Miss Forbes was sitting at the head of the table with two women on either side of her and further down the table two younger women, wearing overalls and caps. The older women eyed Jane, gave her good morning, and Miss Forbes motioned her to a chair next to the older of her companions.

'Sister Soper,' she waved a hand, 'and Sister Cowie.' She nodded at Jane. 'Sister Fox, she came last night, going on duty this evening.' She nodded at the two girls. 'Assistant nurses, Brown and Digby—on day duty—the night staff have their meal when the day staff have taken over.'

Jane, bidden to do so, helped herself to bread and butter and a boiled egg and took the tea she was offered. 'Do you have non-resident staff?' she asked, and was taken aback when Sister Cowie said sharply,

'Certainly not, we manage very well as we are. This isn't like one of your grand teaching hospitals, you know.'

Difficult to answer that one, reflected Jane, and ate her egg, boiled hard and almost cold, while she listened to the others discussing the day's work in a desultory manner. It seemed to her that Miss Forbes knew as much about the patients as the nursing staff. No one spoke to the two girls, who talked almost in whispers between themselves. All very different from her old hospital, decided Jane, but it wouldn't do to judge too hastily and surely there were more nursing staff—probably on the wards already.

The two sisters got up presently, nodded to her briefly and went away, and the girls hurried after them. 'Come up to my office and I'll fit you out with uniform,' said Miss Forbes. 'It may need a bit of altering; you'll have plenty of time to do that today. I'll hand you over to Matron at ten o'clock sharp and she'll take you round the hospital. Dinner is at half-past twelve, tea on the ward and you can make yourself a cup in your place. You'll get a meal at eight o'clock this evening and have a snack meal on the ward or in your office.'

She got to her feet and Jane, who could have eaten a second slice of bread and butter, got up too and followed her out of the room and upstairs and along a narrow corridor to a small room filled with cupboards and lined with shelves laden with linen and blankets.

'Try these,' said Miss Forbes, 'I had no idea what you'd be like—I've done the best I can...'

The blue uniform dress was rather worn and much too large in the waist. Its wearer must have been a woman of very ample proportions, decided Jane, holding it against herself. 'Wants taking in a bit— there's another one and plenty of aprons and caps. Help yourself to a needle and thread.'

It was a far cry from her well tailored uniform at St Cuthbert's but she took it back to her room and sat by the fire with Percy and Simpkin and Bruno crowding round her and, being quite skilful with her needle, contrived to alter one dress to fit her reasonably; the aprons could be pinned and she had her own belt with its silver buckle to cover the pins. The cap was a plain Sister Dora and after the goffered muslin trifle she had worn at her old hospital she found it unattractive. 'Not that it matters,' she assured her companions, 'for I don't know anyone here.'

Matron gave her a cold good-morning when she presented herself at the office. 'I hope you have settled in,' she observed. 'Miss Forbes will have told you the times of meals and so on, I dare say. It remains for me to take you round the hospital.'

There was a well furnished room leading from the hall for the reception of patients and their visitors, Matron's flat and a small room where the records of previous patients were kept, and next to the dining-room was a small, shabbily furnished room with a little gas fire, television and a shelf of books. 'The staff sitting-room,' explained Matron and swept upstairs.

The best rooms, she explained, were at the front of the hospital and were pleasantly furnished and well equipped. Outside each door Jane was told from what each patient suffered and quickly came to the conclusion that almost all the cases were medical and not serious, although there were several convalescent patients from the hospitals in Carlisle. The two-bedded wards weren't as well furnished and were in either wing and the four-bedded ward was at the very end, the beds too close together. There was no television here either and the one window was covered by a net curtain which obscured any view there might be. The occupants of the beds were all old and as they went away Matron said, 'I take one or two geriatrics to oblige their families—so many people these days hold down important jobs and they really haven't the time to spare for elderly relatives.'

How sad, thought Jane, and said nothing, aware that she didn't like Matron. She went back to her cottage and made herself a cup of tea and ate some biscuits and, since there was no one else to talk to, told her companions what she thought of the place. 'Not at all what I expected,' she observed, 'but beggars can't be choosers, can they? And we must make the best of it. Of course I've been silly, I should have accepted the professor's offer, shouldn't I? But you see I couldn't do that, I was getting too interested in him. And that's funny, since I didn't like him over-much at first. Still that's over and done with, isn't it? This afternoon I'm going to find the shops; there must be some not too far away.'

In the dining-room she found the same people who had been at breakfast only this time one of the girls was missing and Matron sat at the head of the table. No one talked much, the meal was eaten quickly and the two older women got up from the table as soon as they had finished and presently the other girl came in and sat down to eat her dinner. It had been a sub-stantial meal, casserole of beef and a milk pudding for afters, and Jane followed Matron out to the corri-dor feeling warm and well fed.

'You are free this afternoon,' said Matron in a voice of one conferring an honour.

'I thought I would take a walk and find the local shops.'

'The nearest shop is twenty minutes' walk. Miss Forbes will get you anything you need.' Matron dis-appeared into her office and Jane went in search of Miss Forbes, whom she found in the kitchen with the untidy girl.

'I've got your milk—you can pay me once a week. You've got a list for the grocer?'

Jane handed it over and went back to collect Bruno. Matron hadn't been very encouraging about finding a shop but an hour's brisk walk would do both herself and Bruno good.

The hospital stood back from a main road, its high wall concealing all but the top floor from it. Jane went through its open gate and turned towards the town's outskirts in the distance. There was no footpath and a good deal of traffic and she decided within the first ten minutes that next time she would go in the other direction in the hope of finding a quieter road. Still, the walk was worth it; she came to a straggling row of small houses with a shop at one end; the kind of shop which sold everything so that she was able to buy a paperback, a magazine or two, dog biscuits, crunchy bits for the cats and a few apples and chocolate. She asked about buses to the town too and wrote down the times she was given; she had enough money for the moment and she didn't think she would need to spend much during the two weeks she was to be on night duty but on nights off she would go into Carlisle and get her account transferred to the bank there.

She walked back with Bruno trotting alongside and in the cottage made tea for herself and then took the cats out before spending a pleasant hour leafing through the magazines until getting into her uniform.

There was only one other person in the dining-room when she got to it—a girl in her late teens who greeted her nervously. She was in uniform and a cap but she wore them as though they didn't belong to her.

'Jane Fox,' said Jane, offering a hand. It was shaken limply.

'I'm Peggy Ash. You're the new night sister...?'

'That's right. Who else is to come?'

The girl sat down opposite her. 'No one. Just us.'

Jane bit back the words on her tongue—a single ward of nearly forty patients, some of whom would be able to do things for themselves and of whom at least some would sleep all night, would be hard work for two nurses, but nearly forty patients, almost all of whom were in separate rooms... 'Are there never more than two night staff?' she asked pleasantly, anxious not to frighten the girl.

'Well, if something happens, like a death or an unexpected admission, then Sister Cowie gets up to help.'

Jane glanced at her watch; if she ate her supper quickly there would be time to go and see Matron. What about a doctor? Was there one on call? And the heavy lifting, the thin girl opposite her didn't look able to lift a year-old baby... her thoughts were interrupted by the entry of Miss Forbes with a macaroni cheese and two covered plates on a tray.

She served the meal, offered hot cocoa from a jug and observed that they could help themselves to second helpings if they wished. 'Your meal for the night is in the plates; you take them with you, and you can make tea in Sister Cowie's office.' She had gone before Jane could say anything.

They finished the macaroni cheese between them, drank all the cocoa and, since there was nothing more to come, Jane said, 'Will you stay here until I come back? I want to see Matron.'

Matron wasn't in her office; Jane tapped on the door marked 'Private' and after a brief pause she was bidden to enter.

Matron lived cosily; the room was well furnished and warm with a bright fire burning, moreover she was sitting at a small table enjoying her supper, which, Jane noted, was a far cry from macaroni cheese— there was a bottle of wine on the table too.

'I'm sorry to interrupt your meal, Matron,' said Jane. 'I wanted to check with you that there are only two of us on duty tonight.'

'I told you that we were short-staffed, Sister Fox. As soon as I can get another nurse I will do so. In the meantime I'm sure you will manage.'

'And a doctor if I should need one in the night?'

'Sister Cowie has his phone number—we try not to disturb him unless it is really necessary. She will give you the report and any further details you may need. If that is all, goodnight, Sister.'

Presently, taking the report from an unfriendly Sister Cowie, Jane reflected that, according to her, none of the patients would need more than the lightest of attention during the night, but once she had hurried away Jane sat down in the tiny office crowded between the rooms at the front of the hospital and read it carefully, asking questions of her companion as she did so.

The girl was willing enough but very vague. Jane got to her feet. 'May I call you Peggy? "Nurse" in front of patients of course. Have you had any training at all?'

Peggy shook her head. 'Only here—there are three of us; the other two are on day duty.'

Jane allowed herself a fleeting thought of the professor; if she had listened to him, sunk her silly pride and made up her mind not to get interested in him, she could have been snugly ensconced with these friends of his. Well, she had cooked her goose and now she must eat it—and a long way from home too.

To Peggy's astonishment she did a complete round, making herself known for a second time to the patients, each of whom, without exception, needed something; flowers removed from the room, fresh water, the bed arranged, a warm drink and, as well as that, while Peggy saw to this, Jane checked the charts and read the care sheets hung on the end of each bed. No one was really seriously ill but several had conditions which needed a sharp eye—three diabetics, two with dangerously high blood-pressure, a post-operative stomach ulcer who looked ill . . .

The two-bedded wards were convalescing gynae cases, all of them youngish, demanding women who took up a good deal of time before she could settle them for the night, and the four-bedded ward took the most time of all—the four old ladies were awake, fretful and needed clean sheets in their beds. Jane rolled up her sleeves and set to with a will, sending Peggy for fresh linens, clean nighties and presently warm drinks and bedpans.

From the look of things, no one had done much for them for hours—something she would discover from the day staff when they came on duty.

They finished at last and Jane said, 'Put the kettle on, Peggy, we're going to have a cup of tea. Is there anything to eat?'

'Just our meal.'

Jane lifted the cover on her plate and studied the contents. Cheese sandwiches and not too many of those. 'I'll bring some biscuits tomorrow night,' she promised.

There might not have been many ill patients but they were kept busy until well after midnight. Not that there were any drugs given by the night staff—the day sister saw to those before she went off duty—but almost all the patients were written up for mild analgesics and minimum sleeping tablets, and, although most of them had declared that they were comfortable when Jane had done her round, their bells pealed every few minutes.

It was almost one o'clock when they sat down to eat their sandwiches and drink more tea and presently Jane set off on another round, this time leaving Peggy in the office.

It wasn't until she reached the old ladies that she found anyone awake. It was another half-hour before she had dealt with bedpans, more clean sheets and a round of warm drinks.

The last old lady to be tucked up again caught her hand in her own bony one. 'Will you be here tomorrow night?' she asked anxiously, and when Jane said yes she went on, 'No one ever bothered to come and see us at night, not after Sister went to her room to have supper; we're not really ill, you see, only old.'

Jane gave the hand a gentle squeeze. 'I'll be here every night, so go to sleep now, my dear; there'll be a nice cup of tea for you in the morning.'

She went back to write the report and drink more tea while Peggy got the trays ready for early morning tea, and then together they began on their early morning chores. The man who had had a partial gastrostomy still looked ill and she took a look at his wound under the pretext that the dressing had become loose. Alternate stitches had been taken out and the area was red and inflamed. She assured the man that everything was going well, re-dressed the wound and took his temperature. She had known that it would be above normal and it was—too high to be ignored. She left him to be made comfortable by Peggy and went along to see to the old ladies. Peggy had given them their tea; she took temperatures and the feeble intermittent pulses, helped them to wash, combed their grey hair and sat them up in their beds. At least they looked alive when she had finished with them and their beds were clean.

Sister Cowie was in a bad temper. She half listened to Jane's report, pooh-poohed the idea of the patient with the infected wound being ill and sneered openly when Jane reported on the old ladies.

'We've enough to do without being bothered overmuch with them,' she said coldly. 'They're only here because their families don't want the bother of them, and they don't pay much.'

Jane was too tired to argue although she said firmly, 'It was only because Matron advised me not to call the doctor unless it was urgent that I didn't ring him, but I expect he'll come when you phone him.'

'Leave that to me, Sister Fox. I'll be off duty this evening; one of the nurses will give you the report.'

Jane wasn't really surprised to see boiled eggs and bread and butter on the table again in the diningroom. She and Peggy ate and wasted no time on small talk—they were too tired and Peggy for one felt dispirited. But by the time she had taken the cats and Bruno for their morning stroll, had a shower and a drink and biscuits by the fire her spirits had risen; she liked a challenge and there was certainly one confronting her.

She took apples, biscuits and the chocolate on duty with her that evening; it had been shepherd's pie for their meal and the sandwiches were fish-paste. There had been no sign of Miss Forbes or Matron and when they got on duty it was to find one of the young nurses waiting for them.

'Who else is on duty?' asked Jane.

'Just me, Sister. Sister Cowie's got an evening off and Sister Soper went early—there's nothing to worry about she said.'

Jane read the report, a series of 'good days' with no details, and unless Sister had forgotten to mention it there had been no doctor's visit. The nurse, when Jane asked, was quite sure that he hadn't called.

Jane went at once to see the patient; he was a quiet elderly man with not much to say for himself but she could see that he was feverish and in pain. A quick look at the wound decided her.

'Peggy, I'll have to depend on you to do a round, just as we did last night; I'll come and join you as soon as I can but there's an ill patient who needs the doctor.'

She phoned the number she had been given, to be told that the doctor was at dinner and didn't wish to be disturbed.

'Fetch him, please,' said Jane in her severest voice. 'It's urgent.'

He sounded impatient but she ignored that, explained the patient's condition and added, 'I won't be responsible for him unless he is seen by a doctor— I think he may have peritonitis.'

He rang off without answering but ten minutes later he came into the room. 'What's all this?' he wanted to know crossly. 'I've had a busy day.'

'And I'm having a busy night, Doctor.'

He gave her an astonished look. 'You're new?'

'Yes. I've taken the dressing down. Here is his chart.'

He went over to the bed and bent over the man and presently straightened. 'Ring for an ambulance, will you, Sister? He will have to go into Carlisle at once.'

He turned back to the man in the bed and spoke reassuringly, and presently he joined her in the office.
'Did you take out the stitches?' he wanted to know.

'I? No. It was my first night on duty last night; I
reported him when I went off duty. I would have
phoned you in the early morning but I was told that
I should only call for anything really urgent.'

He looked away from her. 'Well, I dare say we've
caught it in time.'

The night nearly turned into a nightmare after that.
The ambulance came and the patient was borne away
as quickly as possible. 'I'll go with him,' declared the
doctor. 'They'll need to know—you have his case
sheets?'

She passed them over without a word and, still not
meeting her eyes, he went off after the stretcher.

The commotion had disturbed the patients and
Peggy was flustered and looked near to tears. It took
a long time to settle everyone for the night but the
last old lady was finally settled, they made tea, ate a
biscuit and then went to clear up in the patient's room.
The doctor had said that he would warn the family
and she supposed that Sister Cowie would deal with
the enquiries in the morning. She did another round
in comparative peace and went back to eat the sandwiches and nibble at an apple.

'An hour's peace,' she said hearteningly to Peggy,
who looked as though she ought to be in bed herself.
Five minutes later a bell rang; one of the diabetics
was rapidly become hyperglycaemic...

'A bad night, my dears,' Jane confided to her pets
when she at last got to her cottage, a hard-boiled egg
lying heavy on her insides and the beginnings of a
headache. Sister Cowie had been nasty too. 'Anyone

would think that I had given the poor man peritonitis. Let's hope we settle down for a bit.'

A vain hope; she was a stoic strong girl not given
to self-pity or complaining but the long nights with
too little help and unending chores began to take their
toll. A diet of sandwiches and macaroni cheese alter-
nating with shepherd's pie did nothing to improve
matters. There was no sign of the promised nurse
either. She had had to call the doctor out twice too
and Matron had reproved her for that, refusing to
agree that a mild heart attack could lead to a worse
one and that a diabetic coma sometimes needed a
doctor's intervention. She gave a great sigh of relief
as she and Peggy went down to their breakfast on
their last morning—four whole days off—she could
hardly believe it. It was as she sat at breakfast—boiled
egg again!—that Matron came in to tell her that, as
she had been unable to get a relief nurse, Jane would
have to do at least four more nights.

Jane was unable to utter for a moment. When she
did speak it was in a quiet voice which betrayed
nothing of her feelings.

'I need a rest, Matron. We both do...'

'Oh, there's a girl who will come in while Peggy
has her nights off. Not trained, though, so you will
have to stay, Sister Fox.'

'And if I don't?' asked Jane.

Matron shrugged. 'One of the nurses will have to
go on call as well as do day duty. It is to be hoped
that none of the patients becomes ill during the night.'

Jane thought of the four old ladies, never mind the
convalescents; they would be left to lie in wet beds,
probably unwashed and with no warm drinks if they

woke in the night. She said slowly. 'I will do it, Matron, but under protest.'

'I thought you would see sense,' said Matron. 'You have to think of your cats and dog, don't you?'

Almost a threat, thought Jane.

It was a bitterly cold morning and the cottage was icy. She fed Percy and Simpkin and Bruno and then, wrapped in her coat, she strode out with them for a walk along the frosty grass. They were at the further end when Bruno began to bark very excitedly and ran back the way they had come. Jane turned round to see who it was. Professor van der Vollenhove.

He reached her in a few strides and without preamble observed crossly, 'You tiresome girl, hiding here miles from anywhere—I suppose it's that red head of yours which makes you so impulsive and as for ingratitude...'

He looked at her properly then and said in a quite different voice, 'My dear girl, whatever have they been doing to you?'

Jane burst into tears, unable to choke them back, overjoyed to see him again and at the same time furious with herself for crying.

CHAPTER FIVE

THE professor put a great arm around Jane, heavy but comforting, and offered a large handkerchief. He said in a detached manner, 'You look like a wrung-out dishcloth,' a remark which had the effect of checking her rush of tears.

'So would you,' she said in a fierce watery voice. 'Fourteen nights on duty, meat-paste sandwiches and hard boiled eggs and those poor old ladies and no one bothers, Peggy's a good girl but she hasn't any confidence and she can't lift...'

The professor sighed. It had taken him several days to make up his mind that he would have to find Jane; he had a strong sense of duty and fair play and she had been the subject of neither. He had gone in search of Bessy finally, remembering the address that Jane had mentioned, and had found that good soul unsettled and longing to get away from London. She gave him Jane's address and as soon as he could arrange his work so that he could be away for a couple of days he had driven north. He hadn't known what to expect but Jane's beautiful face, pale and weary, disturbed him.

He considered her impassioned tumble of words for a moment. Then asked, 'Is there somewhere where we can talk?'

'Over there, the little cottage against the wing.'

'Good. Collect up the animals, we'll go there.'

90

She had stopped crying, her nose was pink-tipped and her cheeks were tear-stained but her voice had only the smallest wobble. 'Why are you here?'

She looked at him and saw that he was tired; immaculate, clean-shaven, calm but bone-weary. 'Have you had breakfast?'

'I stopped for coffee.' He was walking her briskly back to the cottage, the two cats and Bruno keeping pace.

She stopped. 'You haven't driven up through the night?'

'I don't have all that amount of time to squander; it was either that or not coming at all.'

'So why did you come?' she frowned. 'And how did you know where I was?'

'I came because you have had enough bad luck through no fault of your own and because you are a nice girl although you are pig-headed.'

He took her by the arm and walked on briskly. 'Bessy gave me your address.'

'I asked her not to tell anyone...'

'She didn't tell me, she wrote it down.' He took the key from her and opened the door and went in after her, with the animals at his heels.

The small room became even smaller with him in it and because he had remained silent she said hastily, 'I'll light the fire and make coffee; the housekeeper here lets us buy things from her.'

He took the matches from her, lighted the fire and turned the flame up high then took off his car coat and hung it on the hook behind the door. Jane had gone into the bedroom to take off her own coat—now she went to put on the kettle. She was still wearing her uniform and turned round at his chuckle. 'That

dress hardly does you justice,' he observed. 'Fortunately you would look nice in a sack.' And then he
asked, 'Why are you blushing?'

'I don't know,' Jane mumbled. She got the two
mugs and the one plate from a shelf, found a spoon,
opened a packet of biscuits and put them on the tin
tray. 'How did you get here? You must have seen
someone in the hospital.'

'The front door was open—there was a large
friendly woman in the hall, and I said I had come to
see you.'

'Miss Forbes. Did she say anything?'

He smiled. 'Yes. "I didn't think it would be long."'
He had been standing; now he urged her into the easy-
chair and took one of the small wooden chairs by the
table. The room was warmer now and the cats and
Bruno were basking in front of the gas fire. The professor drank his coffee, ate most of the biscuits, accepted a second mug and settled back cautiously in
his chair.

'Now, I want to know about your work and this
place—never mind the sandwiches and eggs—how
many patients are there for a start?'

She blew on her coffee. 'Nearly forty.' She de-
scribed the lay-out of the rooms and he nodded.
'Staff?'

'Two sisters and two untrained girls on day duty,
me and another untrained girl—Peggy—on nights.
There's no doctor; at least he comes if it's very urgent
and he's not supposed to be called at nights.'

'You have done that?'

'Yes—the patient was transferred to Carlisle hospital at once. I have had to get him to come twice more.
He doesn't like me . . .'

The professor hid a smile. He asked gravely, 'And your working hours?'

She told him that too and his eyes searched her face. 'You are too tired to go out of doors during the day, aren't you? You have been grossly overworked and I imagine that the patients lack any real nursing care.' He put down his mug. 'How long will it take you to pack?'

'Pack? Me? What do you mean? I've got to go on duty tonight.'

He got up, his head only inches from the ceiling. 'You will come back with me, Jane.' He sounded placid but she could see that he meant every word. 'There is no reason why you shouldn't leave; the hospital has broken its contract with you, if ever there was one, by misrepresentation of the work involved. Impulsive you may be, but I doubt if you would have come all that way if you had known what the working conditions were.' He opened the door. 'So get dressed and get packed, see to the animals and be ready when I get back.'

'Where are you going?'

'To talk to your matron.' He stood by the door, looking at her in her bunchy dress, her hair all over the place and too tired to make sense of anything. He left the door, gave her a quick kiss and went away.

Left alone, Jane tidied away the mugs, tore out of her uniform, showered and got dressed again. She felt bemused by the speed with which everything was happening; she was bemused by the kiss too. 'Out of pity, of course,' she told Bruno. 'I must have looked a perfect fright.'

She did her hair carefully, made up her face nicely and fetched her case from under the bed. The sight of it made the animals restless, so she fetched the baskets and opened them, assuring them that they would be going with her. Where to, she had no idea, and she was far too tired to worry about it.

She was sitting with the cats on her knee and Bruno at her feet, her case packed and her coat ready to put on, when the professor came back. It had been a mistake to sit down of course for she was almost asleep by now but she jerked upright as he came in.

'Ready? Good. Go and say goodbye to Matron; she's in her office. I'll stuff the cats into their baskets—five minutes . . .'

'What did she say? Didn't she object? There's no one to take over from me this evening.'

'Stop fussing. Off you go.'

So she went, rather apprehensive at the idea of seeing Matron.

That lady's beady eyes swept over her with dislike but all she said was, 'It seems that I have no option but to let you go, Miss Fox. Did you know that Professor van der Vollenhove was coming to see you?'

'No, Matron. I hope you find someone to take my place. I'm sorry to leave like that.'

Matron unbent very slightly. 'You are a good worker. The professor very kindly made some suggestions—most helpful—which I shall probably consider. Goodbye, Miss Fox.' She didn't shake hands.

Miss Forbes was in the hall. 'Going? Well, I thought you wouldn't stay long—the one before you only stayed three days . . . I like your young man.'

'He's not my young man,' said Jane, and blushed because she wished that he were, 'just a good friend.'

'"A rose by any other name," ' said Miss Forbes. 'Go along now, don't keep him waiting. I'm going to see Matron and find out what he said. I'll not say any more for this job is my bread and butter but I fancy there'll be changes.' She offered a hand. 'You're such a pretty creature too.'

Jane kissed her cheek. 'You were so kind when I came. I'll not forget that. Goodbye.'

They were waiting for her, the professor with well controlled impatience, Bruno hopefully, and the two cats glaring at her through the little barred windows of their baskets.

As they got into the car Jane said suddenly, 'Ought you to drive? You haven't had any sleep and it's miles.'

'You drive yourself?' asked the professor, getting behind the wheel.

'Yes, of course.'

'Splendid, but do not imagine for one moment that you will be allowed to drive this car. I'm perfectly able to drive you safely back to London.'

'Oh, I know that.' She spoke hastily, afraid that she had offended him. 'I didn't mean that you aren't a good driver...'

His, 'Thank you,' was meek.

They went through Carlisle and presently joined the M6 and Jane closed her eyes and slept, quite unable to keep them open any longer. The professor glanced at her and smiled to himself; despite the careful make-up the shadows under her eyes were dark and she was still pale. Probably when she woke up she would want to know what he had said to Matron. He didn't intend to tell her everything; he occupied the next few miles deciding just what he would leave out, and, that settled, bent his powerful mind to organising the week ahead; he had a number of appointments before he was due to return to Holland as well as a consultation in Edinburgh. He drove on steadily while Jane slept, her head lolling against his shoulder. Just north of Preston he stopped at a small village inn, parked the car and then woke her gently.

She opened her eyes at once and stared up at him. 'Where...?' she began and stopped. She had very nearly made the remark all heroines made in romantic novels; instead she said, 'I've been asleep, so sorry.'

'We're just north of Preston. I came off the motorway—we can have coffee, exercise Bruno and if you have the cats' harnesses we can let them out too. It's quiet here.'

She had tied the harness on to each basket; it was the work of a few minutes to get them out on to the wide grass verge by the side of the narrow road. With the professor and Bruno on his lead, they walked up and down for ten minutes, put the cats back into their baskets and, with Bruno, went in to the inn.

The coffee was hot, and Jane, very much refreshed, felt wide awake. As for the professor, he looked much as he always did, unshakeably calm and apparently without a worry in the world. Only the lines of tiredness were still there.

They drove on presently, back on to the motorway until just north of Birmingham he took the A5. As they drove through Milton Keynes some time later he said, 'We will stop for lunch,' and turned off on to a side-road.

Jane had been asleep again but now she was awake, feeling guilty and hungry too. He drove for a mile or so until they reached a village—Aspley Guise—parked the car by the hotel in the square and invited her to get out.

Free Books Certificate

Yes! Please send me 4 FREE Medical Romances together with my FREE cuddly teddy and mystery gift. Please also reserve a special Reader Service subscription for me. If I decide to subscribe, I will receive 4 brand new books for just £6.80 every month (subject to VAT), postage and packing FREE. If I decide not to subscribe, I shall write to you within 10 days. Any free books and gifts will be mine to keep in any case. I understand that I am under no obligation whatsoever - I may cancel or suspend my subscription at any time simply by writing to you. I am over 18 years of age.

Your Extra Bonus Gift

We all love mysteries, so as well as the books and cuddly teddy we've an intriguing gift just for you. No clues - send off today!

8A3D

Mrs/Miss/Ms/Mr _____
(BLOCK CAPITALS PLEASE)

Address _____

_____

Postcode _____ Signature _____

Offer closes 31st October 1993. The right is reserved to refuse an application and change the terms of this offer. One application per household. Overseas readers please write for details. Southern Africa write to Book Services International Ltd., Box 41654, Craighall, Transvaal 2024. You may be mailed with offers from other reputable companies as a result of this application. Please tick box if you would prefer not to receive such offers. ☐

mps MAILING PREFERENCE SERVICE

No Stamp Needed

Mills & Boon Reader Service
FREEPOST
PO Box 236
Croydon
CR9 9EL

Send No Money Now

Percy and Simpkin were asleep but Bruno got out with them.

The restaurant looked inviting but, hungry though she was, Jane went away to comb her hair and do her face. She looked a fright, she thought, studying her face in the mirror in the Ladies', and she had made no attempt to be an agreeable companion. When she joined him in the restaurant she tried to explain this but he brushed her apologies aside.

He said austerely, 'Idle chatter is the last thing either of us wishes for,' which silenced her while they ordered their meal.

Over the excellent steak and kidney pie they had both chosen she braced herself to ask, 'Where are we going? I mean me and the animals. I'm sure Bessy's sister would have us.'

He offered her a dish of sprouts. 'Bessy's sister has a very small house with two bedrooms; there is barely floor space for Bessy. If you remember I offered you somewhere to stay when I saw you at Lady Grimstone's. The offer still holds good. From the look of you you need a few days of peace and quiet before you look for another job.'

He spoke in a matter-of-fact voice and she had the impression that he considered it no concern of his. He had rescued her from her own impulsive attempt to find work, the friends, whoever they were, would house her until she could get a post in one of the London hospitals and she would be on her own again. And he would forget her...

She ate the excellent jam roll and custard with a complete loss of appetite and when she thanked him his chilly, 'Good, that's settled,' stilled her tongue again.

They went back to the car and he drove back the way they had come until he reached the A1 again. Near Harpenden they joined the M1 and in due course joined the slow-moving queues going into the heart of the city.

They had hardly spoken for some time but now the professor observed, 'We'll be in good time for tea.' He glanced at her. 'You're very tired—without the animals we could have been a good deal quicker.'

She looked out of the window. 'Richmond,' she said. 'Is that where I am to stay?'

'Yes.' He drove towards the river along a side-road, turned in at a wide gateway and stopped before a fair-sized house with white walls, an imposing porch with a wrought-iron balcony above it and large windows already lit in the deepening dusk.

The house door opened as they stopped and a young woman came running out. She poked her head through the window the professor had opened and kissed his cheek and said, cheerfully, 'Here you are, on time too.' She beamed across at Jane. 'Hello, Jane,' she said, 'you must be worn to a rag—and the cats and dog too. Come on in, all of you. Tea is waiting. Rex will be here soon.'

The professor had got out to open Jane's door and put out a steadying hand as she got out. Just like an old woman, she thought crossly. She was aware of the fact that she looked jaded, but did she really need to be reminded that she looked and felt like a crumpled rag?

The professor still held her arm. 'This is Julie——' the kindness in his voice made Jane feel even worse '—married to an old friend of mine. Go inside with her; I'll harness the cats and I'll take them and Bruno for a quick run.'

Julie took her other arm. 'Come on indoors. I wasn't sure what food they eat; just tell me and I'll put out a meal for them.'

She urged Jane into the house, through the wide hall and into a pleasant sitting-room with a splendid view of the river. Jane found herself gently propelled into a small easy-chair. 'A cup of tea and then I'll take you up to your room. We've put you at the back of the house—there's a balcony for the cats and your dog.'

Jane drank her tea, swallowing with it a desire to burst into tears all over her kind hostess, and then followed her up the curving staircase and along a passage with a door at its end. 'We put you here so that you don't have to worry about disturbing us if Bruno barks.' Julie opened the door, disclosing a wide room, charmingly furnished and with doors on to the covered balcony. 'The bathroom's here.' She opened another door. She smiled at Jane. 'Oh, good, Ethel's brought up your case. I'm coming back for you in fifteen minutes. Rex will be back by then and we can all have some tea.'

There was something Jane wanted to know. 'Is Professor van der Vollenhove staying here with you?'

'Nikolaas? Oh, no. He has a dear little mews cottage just behind Brook Street; it's his *pied-à-terre* when he's over here.'

Left to herself Jane washed, did the best she could with her face and hair and got into the grey jersey dress, the only thing which wasn't crumpled by her hasty packing and which she hadn't had a chance to wear at the hospital. She was exploring the balcony when Julie came back.

'Oh, good, you're ready. The men are downstairs—so are your cats and Bruno. They've all had a meal.'

'You're so kind,' began Jane, and was hushed at once by Julie who said,

'Pooh, you'd do the same for me, wouldn't you?'

Jane said that yes, she supposed she would, and followed Julie down the stairs, wishing that she were small and dark and dainty like her.

The men were standing with their backs to the fire talking but they broke off when Julie and Jane joined them.

'Jane, this is Rex; Rex, dear, shake hands and then come and help me get the tea-tray—there's muffins...'

Rex was a thin, scholarly-looking man somewhere in his late thirties, with a long friendly face and thick glasses. He looked clever but kind and he shook her hand firmly before he followed his wife out of the room, leaving Jane facing the professor.

'Feeling better?' he wanted to know. 'These three seem to have settled down happily enough.' He nodded towards Bruno, lying at his feet, wagging his tail in a desultory fashion, and Simpkin and Percy fast asleep side by side.

'You're sure your friends won't mind? It's a frightful imposition...' She glanced at him, gulping back sudden panic. 'I don't know how long it will take to get a job and somewhere to live.'

'You're a great one for rushing your bridges, aren't you? Supposing you spend the next day or two getting back your confidence in yourself. I'll ask around and see if there are any openings for you.'

She said eagerly, 'Will you really? You're very kind—I have been a nuisance. I'm sorry but the hospital at Carlisle sounded all right...'

'And you didn't want to be beholden to me, did you?' He smiled at her and after a moment she smiled back; she couldn't help herself somehow.

Julie and Rex came back followed by a stout middle-aged woman carrying a muffin dish which she set on a trivet by the fire.

'Stay for dinner?' Julie asked the professor.

'I'd like that but I've a dinner engagement.'

'When do you go back to Holland?' Rex asked.

'Tomorrow. I've a lecture to give in the morning—I'll probably get an afternoon plane.'

Jane bent to pat Bruno, pressed against her leg, so that no one should see the surprise and disappointment in her face. The professor glanced at her downbent head and added, 'I've no doubt that Jane will have no trouble in finding a suitable post very shortly.'

'Of course she will,' agreed Julie warmly, 'but for a day or two she's going to have a holiday. I'm dying to hear all about this place in Carlisle. Was it a big hospital? Did you have a ward to look after? I often thought I'd like to have been a nurse only I got married instead.'

'And a good thing too from the patients' point of view,' declared Rex, and everyone laughed.

The professor got up to go presently, he kissed his hostess, patted the two cats and Bruno, and when Jane opened her mouth to thank him once more, said testily, 'Do not, I beg you, thank me again. I hadn't been to that part of England for some years; it made a pleasant break.' He nodded goodbye, gave her a pat

too and went away with his friend, leaving Jane
swallowing indignation heavily laced with despon-
dency at his going.

However, she wasn't allowed to be despondent for
long. Julie seemed determined to spoil her, giving her
a splendid dinner and then telling her kindly to go to
bed. 'For you must be so tired. We'll see to the animals in the morning if you don't feel like getting up.'

So Jane climbed the stairs with the cats and Bruno
trailing behind her and after a blissful hot bath got
into bed. Percy and Simpkin had an old blanket to
sleep on and so had Bruno, but as she dropped off
she was aware that they had all crowded on to her
bed and curled up beside her. When she woke up in
the morning Percy was lying as heavy as lead on her
chest, staring at her. The other two were on the
balcony, peering out at the garden below. She got out
of bed and went to look too; it was a pretty garden
even in winter with the curve of the river in the distance. There was a flat green meadow on the opposite
bank; it reminded her that Holland was flat too. The
professor would be there soon and she wondered
where. Lady Grimstone had never mentioned a wife
but perhaps he had one; she would very much like to
know that. 'Although there is no point,' she observed
to Simpkin. 'The whole idea of going away was so
that I would have nothing to do with him and here I
am bothering about where he lives. But I do wonder
what he's doing.' Simpkin yawned. 'Probably still in
bed, snoring his handsome head off,' finished Jane
crossly.

She might not have felt so ill tempered had she
known that he was thinking about her. His thoughts

had not a spark of romance among them but certainly they had to do with her future.

The next three days were quite perfect; the animals settled down as though they had lived there all their lives, Julie fed her as though she had been starving, went through the contents of her wardrobe with her and demanded to know about the hospital, and somehow Jane found herself telling her about cousin Basil too and her grandmother and Bessy. 'And I wondered if you'd mind very much if I went to see her? Only I can't take the animals; even Bruno is a bit of a problem on buses...'

'I'll drive you. We'll go this afternoon. Ethel will keep an eye on the cats and Bruno can come in the car.'

Bessy's sister's house was one of a row of small red-brick cottages all exactly alike, with no front gardens and shabby paintwork. Jane's heart sank when she saw it but she got out when Julie said she would stay in the car with Bruno, and knocked on the door.

It was Bessy who opened it and at the sight of her burst into tears. 'Miss Jane—well, I never did, what a sight for sore eyes.' She mopped her face and Jane gave her a hug and was urged into the narrow little hall.

'Me sister's out—she does for several ladies up west. Come on in, I'll make a cup of tea.'

'A friend brought me, Bessy; she's outside in the car with Bruno.'

'Well, they can come in too. You fetch them while I pop on the kettle.'

Bessy looked doubtfully at Julie as she came into the cramped front room with Bruno, but Julie, despite her beautiful clothes and air of wealth, could put anyone at ease. They sat, the three of them with Bruno on Jane's knee, drinking the strong dark tea which Bessy made.

Jane made light of her stay in Carlisle. 'I'm looking for a job in London, Bessy. If I get something suitable and can find a little flat would you come and share it with me?'

'Oh, Miss Jane, that'd be 'eaven.'

'It's different from Granny's house, isn't it? You miss the village . . . ?'

'That I do, Miss Jane. Me sister's ever so good but you can't pop yer 'ead out of doors 'ere for a breath of fresh air, for there ain't any.'

'Oh, Bessy, I do know what you mean—perhaps I could get a post in a smaller hospital somewhere in the country. It might be easier to find somewhere to live for a start and far better for the animals.'

'They'm all right, Percy and Simpkin . . . ?'

'Fine. Mrs Ferguson has kindly offered all of us a home until I can start work.'

'And 'ow did you get back from that place, then?'

Jane had managed not to mention the professor but now she had to. With a slightly heightened colour she said casually, 'Oh, Professor van der Vollenhove— you remember him, Bessy? He was kind to us when we left Granny's—drove me back to London.'

'Fancy that now. Being a doctor I suppose 'e goes to all the hospitals round about.'

'He's gone back to Holland,' said Jane, and something in her voice made her companions look at her, though neither of them spoke.

They drove back to Richmond presently and Jane said as they went into the house, 'If you don't mind,

Julie, I'll go to as many nursing agencies as possible tomorrow and see if I can get something. I'll get the nursing magazines too and apply for anything that looks promising.'

'Your old hospital can't take you?'

Jane shook her head. 'That was the first thing I did when Basil told us to leave. They were awfully nice, but there wasn't anything—they'd filled my job, of course, months ago as soon as I had to leave.'

'I dare say that's best. You certainly already look much better and if you feel ready for work again... Go by Underground once the morning rush-hour is over.' She paused. 'What am I thinking of? Rex will be going up to the City around nine o'clock; go with him and come back when you like. Don't worry about the animals. I'll keep an eye on them.'

Jane thanked her. She would have to decide on something soon; the nicest person in the world couldn't be expected to house the four of them for more than a few days.

Rex set her down in Oxford Street and she set about calling at as many agencies as she could find. She had armed herself with the *Nursing Mirror* and the *Nursing Times* and, after several agencies, over coffee she scanned the offers of work in them.

There were several which looked promising but the trouble was it would take time even if she could get accepted, what with references and appointments.

She would put her name down at as many agencies as possible for temporary work and apply for a hospital post at the same time. Where she would live was a question to be worried about later.

She went back to Richmond during the afternoon, told Julie of her plans, took Bruno for a brisk walk

and then sat down to answer the most suitable jobs.
It took her the rest of the evening and she went to
bed feeling that at least she had made a start. She
woke in the night, though, and began to worry about
the animals and Bessy. Even if everything was
straightforward, it would take two or three weeks
before she could expect to take up a permanent job
in any of the larger hospitals. She reviewed her fi-
nances; she had received no money from the hospital
in Carlisle as yet, she still had her five hundred pounds
intact and a good deal of the money she had earned
at Lady Grimstone's; perhaps it would be enough to
rent a room somewhere—on the ground floor because
of the cats and Bruno—for as long as it would take
to get settled permanently. The future, viewed in the
small hours of the night, didn't look very promising,
but when she woke in the morning a watery sun was
shining and the animals were sitting in a tidy row on
the balcony enjoying it and the world didn't seem such
a bad place after all. 'I'm getting soft,' she told them
as she got out of bed to drink her morning cup of tea
in their company. 'I'm perfectly able to cope, I shall
get a splendid job and we'll all live happily ever after.'

Percy was the only one who bothered to look at
her and that with a scornful yellow eye.

She took Bruno for his walk directly after breakfast
and came back glowing with the exercise and, since
Ethel was really proud of her polished floors, she went
in through the little gate at the side of the back garden
and in by the kitchen door. Here she stopped to wipe
Bruno's paws, take off her rather muddy shoes and
walk through to the hall.

Julie was there, standing on the bottom stair,
leaning over the banisters talking to the professor, who

was standing in the middle of the hall, still in his car coat.

Bruno gave a bark of pleasure and trotted to greet him but Jane stayed where she was.

'Hello,' said the professor pleasantly, but showing no special pleasure at seeing her. She waited for him to add, 'Still here?' but he didn't.

It was Julie who spoke. 'Oh, good, you're back, Jane. Do take Nikolaas into the drawing-room and entertain him for a bit—I'm going through the linen cupboard and if I don't finish it now I'll never get the energy to do so.'

She didn't wait for an answer but disappeared up the stairs so that Jane, still in her coat and with her shoes in her hand, felt compelled to move into the hall.

The professor remained silent; he took her shoes from her, glanced at her stockinged feet, laid the shoes down on the floor and went to open the drawing-room door. He had cast off his car coat and as she went past him he slid hers from her shoulders and tossed it after his, waited while Bruno bustled after Jane and then closed the door after him and leaned against it.

'Well?' he asked genially.

She turned to face him. 'I'm still here,' she began, and thought what a silly remark that was. 'I've applied for six jobs and got my name down at several agencies for temporary work while I wait for the replies. And I've been to see Bessy.'

'Is she happy?' He hadn't moved from the door so she stayed where she was.

'I don't think so; you see Stepney isn't anything like Dorset, is it?'

He agreed gravely. 'Have you any plans for her?'

'Well, if I can get a good post at one of the hospitals here I could rent a small flat and she could come and live with me—it's the next best thing...'

He left the door and strolled across the room to stand before her.

'The best thing, however, Jane, is for you to marry me.'

CHAPTER SIX

JANE opened her mouth to speak and then closed it
again. Without her shoes she had even further to look
up into the professor's face, but there was nothing in
it to indicate if she had dreamt his words—perhaps
he was joking...

She tried again. 'What did you say?'

'I asked you to marry me.' He smiled gently down
at her. 'Believe me, I have given the matter some
thought and I consider it to be a most suitable
arrangement.'

'Why?'

He didn't answer her directly. 'We got off to a bad
start, didn't we? But we suit each other very well, you
know. We have much in common and since you have
been in the nursing profession you know, none better,
the kind of life a medical man leads and would be
prepared to put up with delayed meals, sudden depar-
tures and long absences. I have an excellent housekeeper in Holland but I need a wife to entertain my
friends and fend off too much social life. My work
means a great deal to me, Jane, but I need someone
to come home to—not, I must emphasise, someone
simply agog to go dancing and dining and entertain-
ing but someone who will listen if I need to talk. Does
all that sound very selfish to you?'

'No. It's sensible and honest. Only it wouldn't do.
You aren't in love with me, are you? Besides, people
who marry love each other...'

'No, I'm not in love with you, nor do I love you—
two different things, I must point out. One falls in
and out of love but when one loves that is an entirely
different matter, for that lasts through life and beyond
and is a rare thing. Putting the romantic aspect on
one side, I hope that you will consider the matter. I
am in England for the next two weeks and I shall see
you as often as possible.' He took her hand in his and
she felt its cool firmness. 'Will you come with me
now? I have to go home before I go to the hospital.
We can lunch together and we won't say any more
about this unless you want to.'

'Even if I . . . that is, I can't leave Bessy and Bruno
and Percy and Simpkin.'

'Of course not. They can all come too.'

'To Holland?'

'Yes. Bessy will have her country life again and I
have no doubt that the cats and Bruno will settle down
very well.'

He spoke bracingly and in a matter-of-fact manner
which made it all sound easy. She had only to say
yes . . .

Julie came in then followed by Ethel with the coffee.

'Sorry I've been so long.' She beamed at them both.
'How long are you here for, Nik?'

'Two weeks, most of them here in London. I'm
going to take Jane home with me for lunch presently.
You won't mind if we leave the cats here? Bruno will
go with us.'

'Of course I don't mind. I hope you'll have some
free time so that you can take Jane out and around . . .'

'I intend to.' He glanced over at Jane. 'If she agrees
to that.'

Jane wondered what would happen if she said that no, she disagreed. She had no doubt that the professor, being the man he was, would ride, in the nicest possible way, roughshod over her objections.

She murmured suitably and took herself off to fetch a coat, rearrange her hair and add a little more lipstick. She had no idea where they were going for lunch; the grey jersey—such a useful dress and how tired she was of it—would pass muster. Winter white would be nice for a wedding outfit... She gave a shocked look at her reflection; she had no intention of agreeing to the professor's ridiculous proposal. Probably he was tired after his journey and hadn't meant a word of it.

She had no way of telling. When she went downstairs again he got his coat, invited Bruno to accompany them and urged her to get into the car.

'Have a nice lunch,' said Julie, and waved them away before going to the kitchen to have more coffee and confide in the faithful Ethel that the professor seemed to have his eye on Miss Fox.

'And about time too,' said Ethel, 'for a nicer young lady I've yet to meet and it's high time he wed—ten years or more I've known him and never anything but his blessed work.'

The professor drove back into London, through Fulham and South Kensington until he reached Park Lane and turned away into the quiet streets lined with large silent houses, to turn down a narrow road and into a mews—half a dozen cottages with immaculate paintwork and tubs of miniature conifers on either side of their doors. He drove to the end cottage and stopped.

Jane looked at his face enquiringly.

'I have had this place for some time now, it is convenient for me to have somewhere to live when I am over here for I come and go quite frequently and often at a moment's notice. I can come and go as it suits me, for Slocombe looks after it for me. Come in and meet him.'

Slocombe was at the door as they reached it, a bright-eyed, white-haired man, a little stooped but spry in his movements. He greeted the professor with the respectful familiarity of an old servant and, when Jane offered a hand, took it with just the right amount of deference.

'Show Miss Fox where she can tidy herself, will you, Slocombe? We'll have lunch in ten minutes.'

She was led away down the narrow little hall to a cubby hole of a cloakroom which nevertheless held everything anyone needing to refurbish her person might need. Jane smoothed her already smooth head of glowing hair, added a little more lipstick and went a little uncertainly into the hall. There were two doors on either side of it, one of them half open and at which the professor appeared. 'In here, Jane—come and have a glass of sherry...'

The room was surprisingly large, running from back to front of the cottage and taking up the whole of one side. There wasn't a great deal of furniture in it but every chair and table, cupboard and sofa was exactly right for its size. Jane, bidden to sit, chose a small armchair, upholstered in wine-coloured velvet, and the professor set her glass on a small piecrust table beside it. There was a small fire burning in the grate and several lamps shed a pleasant glow against the grey day outside. The professor might be a hard-working man, reflected Jane, but when he wasn't working he lived comfortably enough. It was a pity that she didn't know a little more about him ... She glanced up and caught his eye and, as though he had read her thoughts, he observed in a matter-of-fact way, 'Of course we shall have to get to know each other, shall we not?'

'Well, I don't know,' she mumbled awkwardly.

'Understandably,' he observed briskly. 'Our previous meetings have been either of an urgent or a tearful nature, but I hope that over the next week or so we may get to know each other in more normal circumstances.'

'Yes, but even if I—that is, even if we married, supposing it didn't work out? We might dislike each other, you might fall in love with someone.'

'Jane, I am thirty-nine years old, I have had my fill of falling in and out of love and for the last five years or so I have been perfectly content with my life and my work. It is much more likely that you will find a man you will be happy with, in which case we will deal with the situation, should it arise, in a civilised manner. You can dismiss this nonsense of disliking each other. I didn't race around the country looking for someone I disliked; I was looking for someone I regard as a good friend.' He smiled suddenly and she found herself smiling back at him. 'You don't dislike me?'

'I like you very much,' said Jane in a small voice. Being an honest girl, she added, 'Although you do annoy me sometimes.'

'Which should add a touch of spice to our relationship,' said the professor easily.

Slocombe came then to bid them to lunch, and they crossed the hall to the dining-room, one of the two rooms on that side of the cottage.

'The other door is to my study,' said the professor, ushering her into a small room facing the mews. It was a small apartment but furnished with great good taste. There was a fire burning here too in front of which sat a large black cat, well fed and sleek but with a rather battered appearance.

'Hannibal,' said the professor as they sat down at the circular table. 'Don't ask me why—Slocombe knows—but he chose to come and live with us and he needed a name.'

'He's rather war-torn . . .'

'A great fighter in his day, I should imagine,' and as Slocombe came into the room he asked him, 'Why do we call Hannibal by such a name, Slocombe?'

'He is a cat who has undoubtedly fought his way through life, sir. It seemed a fitting name.'

Slocombe served the soup and went away and Jane said, 'Does he run this house for you without any help?'

'Mrs Crockett comes in every morning to do what I believe is called the rough, otherwise Slocombe deals with everything.'

Jane spooned soup—parsnip and apple and delicious. 'And in Holland?' she ventured. 'Does he go there with you?'

'No need, I have an excellent housekeeper and man there.' He looked at her, smiling again. 'I think you do not know where I live: between Amsterdam and Hilversum—a very small village by a large lake. Utrecht is about twelve miles to the south and since I work in all three cities it is very convenient—it is also very quiet, a short distance from the motorway but quite unspoilt. I think that you will like it there.'

Slocombe handed a ragout of chicken of such excellence that Jane wondered if he was a cordon bleu cook and as if to leave her in no doubt about it he followed that with a fresh lime tart with strawberry sauce.

They went back to the sitting-room for their coffee with Bruno sitting between them, drowsing before the fire. Jane, casting her mind back to the hospital at Carlisle, was unable to suppress a shudder.

The professor, observing her from his chair, remarked cheerfully, 'Are you thinking about that hospital? Well, don't. Try and forget it.'

'I can't help thinking about those old ladies—and the matron was a horrid woman.'

'Oh, I agree with you there. I dare say that she will mend her ways...'

'What did you say?'

'Oh, not a great deal—mentioned one or two names, asked when the place had last been inspected, pointed out that it would be a pity to close the place for lack of staff.'

Jane sat up straight. 'You did? Oh, I am glad—how very nice of you...'

'There was nothing nice about it,' said the professor testily, 'merely an unpleasant duty.'

She felt snubbed and wished that she had a ready answer for that but, since none was forthcoming, she asked rather stiffly, 'You only came back to England this morning? Am I interfering with your plans, Professor?'

He glanced at his watch. 'I have a patient to see at half-past three and no, you are not interfering with my plans—you were part of them.'

'Oh, was I?'

He settled back in his chair. 'I shall have to be at the hospital tomorrow but I will call for you in the evening—would eight o'clock suit you?—we can have dinner together and take a further opportunity to get to know each other.'

'I'm not sure if that is a good idea——' began Jane cautiously, to be ruthlessly interrupted by him.

'My dear girl, unless we see more of each other how will you decide to marry me?'

'What about you? I mean, you have to decide, too.'

'I have already done so. Have I not proposed to you? Something not lightly undertaken, I can assure you.'

Which seemed unanswerable.

He took her back presently, carrying on a vague conversation which had nothing to do with themselves, and it was only as he stopped before Julie's house that he observed, 'When you have made up your mind we might go and see Bessy; she might need a little time to think things over.'

He didn't stay long; his consulting-rooms were in Harley Street, not too far away, but it was already three o'clock. He kissed Julie's cheek, touched Jane briefly on the shoulder and went away.

'What a busy man,' observed Julie lightly. 'When are you seeing him again?'

'He is taking me out to dinner tomorrow evening.' Jane came to a sudden halt. 'I can't go—I've nothing to wear...'

'If you have any money at all, now is the time to spend it,' declared Julie as she eyed Jane's splendid person. 'A little black frock is quite out of the question for you—blue, that lovely dark blue they call Prussian—I know just the shop, we'll go in the morning...'

Jane, suddenly careless of a thrifty future, agreed.

The dress, when they found it, was exactly right; it was also a good deal more money than Jane had intended to pay but she thrust aside gloomy thoughts of a rainy day and bought it. It was worth every penny, of course, its rich blue silk setting off her charming figure to its very best advantage. The neck was square and low-cut, the sleeves long and tight with a row of little buttons at the wrists, and its wide skirt was discreetly mid-calf in length, something which she and Julie and the sales lady agreed was entirely suitable for her.

'I'm too big to wear a very short skirt,' said Jane almost apologetically, and was comforted by the sales woman assuring her that the longer skirt was coming back into favour. 'Besides,' she had added smoothly, 'madam has a lovely figure and this dress shows it off to perfection.'

Jane, handing over a great deal of money, hoped the professor would be of the same opinion. Not, she reflected, that that had anything to do with this idea of his. It had its temptations: a secure future for herself, Bessy and the animals, no more worries about money, no need to work, to find somewhere to live, to pinch and save with an eye to the future. She told herself that she hadn't made up her mind, indeed, she would probably refuse him: a high-handed decision and flying in the face of Fate, who disliked being interfered with and decided forthwith to do something about it.

She dressed in good time and, with her face nicely made up and her hair brushed into its shining chignon, she went downstairs to wait for the professor.

He arrived punctually, spent ten minutes or so chatting with Julie and Rex, made much of Bruno, and the cats and then suggested that they should go, helped Jane into her coat without saying a word about the dress and popped her into the car.

She was a well-brought-up girl and though she seethed with annoyance at his lack of interest in her person she maintained a polite conversation as they drove away from Richmond. She petered out presently and he said, 'You don't have to be polite with me, Jane, and isn't it time you called me Nik?'

'I'm sure I don't know what you mean,' said Jane coldly, 'but if you prefer to be silent, I don't mind in the least.'

'Oh, good. I've had a busy day and just to sit beside you and unwind is exactly what——' He broke off as the car ahead of them careered across the street, mounted the pavement and ploughed into a group of people standing there. He had brought the car to a halt before Jane could utter so much as a squeak. 'First-aid kit is in the back pocket,' he said in a quite ordinary voice. 'Get it and come after me. Shut the car door.'

He was out of his seat and across the street to the horrible mêlée on the pavement, leaving her to do as he had told her. She found the first-aid kit, closed the doors carefully and sped after him.

There were several people lying on the pavement and, as far as she could make out, two still in the car, tilted crazily on its side. As if by magic a small crowd had gathered but shuffled back when the professor, in no uncertain voice, bade them to do so. 'Someone ring for the police and an ambulance; the rest of you keep well back so that we can see who is hurt.'

He was on his knees beside a woman who was badly cut by glass and took the kit from Jane without a word. It was no time to waste with words, anyway. She collected up several of the injured who weren't badly hurt and sat them against the brick wall of the empty warehouse they had been passing and then, at the professor's call, went to bandage a small girl's cut leg and tie a sling around her bigger brother's broken arm. By that time the police had arrived and so had an ambulance and after them the fire brigade. It took time to get the two people out of the car and Jane, wrapping her own coat around the shoulders of an old woman, who was shivering with shock and cold, saw the professor bending over them as they were laid on the stretchers and then talking to the young doctors who had come with the ambulance. He was in his shirt-sleeves now and she wondered what had happened to his jacket. She allowed her thoughts to dwell for a moment on his elegance in a dinner jacket and cast an eye down on her own dress.

It was ruined. She had knelt on the pavement and several people had bled all over the skirt and across the bodice. She registered the fact numbly, for it didn't seem important in the face of the chaos around her. A chaos which was being rapidly dealt with, the ambulances loading up the victims and speeding away, the police dispersing the crowd, the fire rescue truck gone and a breakdown truck taking its place.

What a lot can happen in an hour, thought Jane as she saw the last stretcher loaded and borne away. There were only police now and the professor, getting into his jacket in an unhurried manner as he talked to them and then came towards her.

'Where's your coat?' he wanted to know. 'You'll catch your death of cold.'

'There was an old woman,' she mumbled. 'Will they be all right? The people who were injured?'

'Difficult to say at this stage. The driver had a heart attack, I should imagine; the passenger has concussion. Mostly broken arms and legs.'

He had taken off his jacket again and was putting it around her shoulders.

'Don't do that, you'll spoil it,' said Jane wildly. 'My dress is covered in blood . . .' She burst into tears. 'It's ruined. I—I only bought it this morning . . .' She gave a great sniff. 'What a pig I am to worry about it while all these poor people are . . .'

The professor's voice was very gentle. 'Such a pretty dress too, and you so beautiful in it, Jane.' He mopped her face and put an arm around her.

'Yes, it was, and I won't be able to go out with you again because I can't afford to buy another one . . .'

'It looks as though you'll have to marry me after all so that I can buy you one just like it.'

He had urged her back to the car and shoved her gently into it and, after a final word with one of the policemen, he got in beside her. Before he drove away he picked up the phone, explained to Claridge's, reversed the car and went back the way they had come.

Slocombe came from the kitchen as they entered the professor's house and, with the air of a man whom it was impossible to disconcert or surprise, took his

jacket from Jane's shoulders, observed in calm tones
that he presumed there had been some kind of an accident and listened poker-faced as his master recommended that he took Miss Fox upstairs to the guest
room and found her a dressing-gown. 'You will feel
much better after a warm bath,' he added to her, and
gave her a gentle shove in the direction of the stairs.
'And can you find us something to eat, Slocombe,'
he added, 'in about an hour's time?'

'Leave it to me, sir,' replied the paragon. 'It is to
be hoped that your car is not damaged.'

'No, no, I'll give you the details later.'

Slocombe nodded in a dignified way and led Jane
upstairs to a small bedroom at the back of the cottage,
opened the door to reveal an even smaller bathroom,
complete in every luxurious detail, indicated that he
would be back with a suitable garment for her to wear,
and left.

The room was charming but Jane didn't waste time
exploring it; she got out of the dress and examined it
carefully; it was indeed ruined; moreover she had lost
her coat. As she waited for the bath to fill she did
some mental arithmetic with rather depressing results
but the warm, scented water did much to revive her
spirits. She got into her undies again and went back
into the bedroom and found a dark blue thin wool
dressing-gown laid on the bed. She was a big girl but
since it was one of the professor's it swallowed her
whole and she was forced to hitch it around her waist
by its cord and turn the sleeves up. Even with her hair
neatly pinned she looked like a scarecrow. Clutching
the garment round her so as not to trip up in her shoes,
she took a look around her. It was definitely a
woman's room; pastel pinks and blues, the bed very

prettily covered by a quilted spread and silk curtains at the windows. There were combs and brushes on the dressing-table too and silver-topped jars, and the bottles contained a variety of make-up. Jane frowned and went cautiously downstairs.

The professor was waiting for her and, but for a faint twitch at the corner of his really firm mouth, he betrayed none of the amused delight at the sight of her, and Jane, expecting some joking reference to her appearance, relinquished the haughty lift of her chin and gave him a shy smile.

'Come and sit by the fire,' invited the professor at his most urbane. 'We have plenty of time for a drink before Slocombe finds us something to eat. I'm sorry our evening has been spoilt—so we must try again some time and hope for better luck.'

He rambled on, putting her at her ease, until Slocombe, looking both benevolent and smug, summoned them to the dining-table. He had every right to be smug; there were potted shrimps and wafer-thin brown bread and butter, lamb chops done in the French style wth a sauce of French mustard and wine vinegar, a potato purée with garlic and cream and mushrooms with tarragon and by way of afters *crème fraiche* with black cherries.

When he brought in the coffee tray the professor said, 'Very nice, Slocombe—I knew I could rely on you.'

'A pleasure, sir.'

He arranged the coffee-cups just so and Jane said warmly, 'That was a delicious meal, Slocombe. I don't know how you managed it so unexpectedly...'

'Thank you, miss, I endeavour to be prepared for any eventuality...'

They were back in the sitting-room with Hannibal curled up on Jane's lap when the phone rang. The professor listened, said, 'I'll be with you in ten minutes,' and got up. 'I have to go to the hospital.' He paused and put an encouraging hand on her shoulder. 'Slocombe shall drive you back to Julie's.'

He didn't apologise, but she didn't expect him to: this, if they were to marry, would be the pattern of their days...

She heard him speak to Slocombe and a moment later leave the house as Slocombe came into the room. 'Would you wish to return now, miss? Or shall I drive you back later?'

'Oh, I think straight away, thank you, Slocombe. Would the professor mind if I wore this?' She plucked at the over-sized garment in which she was swathed. 'My dress is a bit messy.'

'Certainly, miss, and, if I might suggest, I will fetch a jacket for you to wear as well. It is cold outside. If you will wait for a moment I will fetch the car.'

He did appear again shortly bearing a car coat of the professor's into which he helped her. She must look a sight, she reflected, following him out to a trim little Mini drawn up outside the door.

Slocombe drove well and at that time of the late evening there wasn't much traffic about. As she prepared to get out at Julie's house, she said, 'It is very kind of you to drive me back. Would you like to come in? I could give you back these things then if you waited a moment...'

'That would be convenient if it is no trouble, miss. A disappointing evening for you and the professor. It is to be hoped that you will be more fortunate at a later date.' He spoke stiffly but she sensed that he liked her. He was, she guessed, a man who would never step out of his allotted place in life. He was nice all the same—she wondered if the professor realised what a treasure he had.

They went indoors and Julie came to meet them from the drawing-room. 'My dear Jane—what has happened? You're not hurt? Where's Nik?'

Jane explained quickly and Rex, following her out into the hall, took Slocombe away for a drink while Jane hurried upstairs and got into the grey dress, folded the dressing-gown and jacket tidily and took them down to him. He took them with dignity, bade her goodnight, bowed to Julie and Rex and took himself neatly away.

'What a treasure that man is,' said Julie, echoing Jane's earlier thoughts. 'Now come in and tell us just what has happened.'

'How awful—all those poor people . . . your dress? Is it spoilt?'

'Hopelessly.'

'And where is your coat? You were wearing it when we saw you leave here.'

'I gave it to an old woman who was cold and shocked.'

'Quite right too,' said Julie. 'You've had supper? A meal of sorts? Good. You're going to bed and Ethel shall bring you some warm milk.'

Which Jane did and, although she thought she wouldn't sleep thinking about the accident, she dropped off at once.

It was an hour or so later when the professor telephoned Julie.

'She's tucked up in bed an hour since. I'm sorry you had such a beastly evening.'

He dismissed that. 'Her dress—do you know where she bought it? You do—good. See if you can replace it, will you, and send me the bill? Oh, and her coat— do something about that too, will you?'

'Yes, of course, but will she mind?'

'Since we are to marry I don't see that she can object.'

'Nik—you mean that? That's wonderful. I wonder why Jane didn't tell us this evening?'

She heard him laugh. 'She doesn't know yet,' he said and hung up.

Jane had half expected to hear from him during the next day but since there was no word from him by teatime she took Bruno for a long walk, groomed the cats and settled down for a quiet evening with Julie and Rex. She went to bed early, quite put out, half determined to pursue her efforts to find a job, telling herself that she had no intention of listening to the professor's preposterous proposal, but when she got up the next morning and went to look out of the window and open the door on to the balcony it was to see the professor strolling round the side of the house. He looked up and saw her.

'Good, you're awake. Hurry up and dress and eat breakfast. I've got a morning off—we'll go and see Bessy.'

She opened her mouth to protest and he added, 'No, don't fuss, there's a good girl.'

'You'll get cold down there,' said Jane.

'Is that an invitation to come up?' He gave her a wicked grin and she shut the door with a snap.

She got into the tweed suit and a woolly jumper; Julie had murmured something about getting a coat and she had half planned to go to Marble Arch and see what there was in Marks & Spencer's; now she would have to make do with her raincoat. Not in the best of tempers, although she was aware of pleasure at the thought of seeing the professor again, she went downstairs.

The two men were already at the table; they both stood up as she went in, settled her between them, plied her with coffee, scrambled eggs and toast and told her to be quick and eat them.

'Julie will be down in a minute,' said Rex. 'Are you going to take Bruno with you?'

'I haven't decided to go yet...' began Jane, put out at being taken for granted.

'Of course you are coming,' said the professor in a no-nonsense voice and smiled at her, and she stared back at him, struck dumb by the knowledge that she would go anywhere he wanted her to go just as long as he was with her. Did one fall in love while eating toast and marmalade, she wondered wildly, and why hadn't she known about it sooner? She had had ample time; she had felt only the faint stirrings of excitement when he had proposed and she had squashed those immediately. It altered everything, of course—he had asked her to marry him and now she knew that she loved him it would be perfectly all right for her to do so. That there might be difficulties she brushed aside. Love conquered all, didn't it?

She said in a calm voice, 'Yes, I'll come,' and when Julie came into the room joined in the conversation in a perfectly normal voice with a serene face. Only her green eyes shone like emeralds. The professor, an observant man, decided that it was because she was excited at the prospect of seeing Bessy again.

They left as soon as breakfast finished and despite the rush-hour traffic were outside the little house in Stepney by ten o'clock. Bessy was alone and delighted to see them.

'Well, now,' she declared, 'what a treat for sore eyes, an' Bruno too—come on in and we'll have a cuppa. Me sister's doing for a lady over in West 'am—an all-day job. I'm thinking of doing a bit of cleaning meself, for I don't know what ter do with me days.'

Sitting in the cold little front parlour presently, drinking their tea, she asked, 'Got a job yet, Miss Jane?' She glanced at the professor drinking his tea, strong, with tinned milk and too much sugar, with every appearance of enjoyment.

'Jane is going to marry me,' he said calmly, and ignored Jane's quick breath. Without looking at her he took her hand, lying on the table beside his, and held it in a firm comforting grasp. 'And that is why we have come to see you, Bessy. Would you like to come to Holland and live with us? There is plenty for you to do there and we shall live in the country. Bruno and Percy and Simpkin will come too and when we come over to England you can come too and pay a visit to your sister here.'

Bessy sat open-mouthed. 'You'm not joking, sir? Gospel truth, is it?'

'Gospel truth, Bessy. Talk it over with your sister and let us know what you think about it.'

'What about me bit of money? Can I take it with me?'

'There's no reason why not. Of course you will have the same wages as everyone else in my home.'

'Well, I don't need to take me time about that, sir. I'll come and gladly. Me and me sister get on a treat but she's got 'er friends and don't need me, as you might say.'

'Splendid. We shall be going in about two weeks' time and we will let you know all the details in plenty of time. Can you get a passport?'

Bessy looked doubtful. 'I'll 'ave ter ask...'

'I'll help you, Bessy. I'll come and see you in a day or two and see to things for you,' Jane told her, and looked with surprise across the table at the professor. Here she was agreeing to everything he had suggested and she still hadn't made up her mind. It had, she reflected with a touch of peevishness, been made up for her.

CHAPTER SEVEN

THEY took leave of an excited and happy Bessy presently and as Jane got into the car she reflected that being in love with the professor had apparently rendered her powerless to disagree with anything he said. Indeed, she seemed to have to agree to everything he had suggested although she wasn't at all sure that she had actually agreed to marry him.

'That's settled,' said the professor in a no-nonsense voice as he got in beside her and drove off. 'Now all that is needed is for you to give me a date and tell me where you wish to marry.'

'I hadn't thought about it,' said Jane faintly.

'Well, do so now. You prefer a church? Good, so do I. Would it not be convenient if we were to marry at the last possible moment? I have a number of appointments to fit in during the next two weeks and if you would agree we could marry and leave for Holland on the same day.'

He was driving west through the city and she wondered where they were going. 'Have I actually said that I would marry you?' she asked.

'Perhaps not in so many words. Will you marry me, Jane?'

It might prove a disaster but she was prepared to rise to that. Being in love made one careless of the consequences and perhaps in time his liking for her would turn into something deeper. 'Yes,' said Jane loudly, 'I will.'

'Good.' He took a turning just before they reached
Harrods, into a network of narrow streets lined with
smart boutiques.

Jane peered out of the window. 'Oh, this is where
Julie brought me . . .'

He didn't answer but got out of the car and opened
her door, took her arm and marched her into the shop.

The blue dress was lying enticingly across a small
gilt chair in the elegant showroom and the sales lady
she had seen previously advanced into the shop to meet
them. She greeted them effusively, adding, 'I have
been most fortunate, sir—this is precisely the same
model as that which madam bought the other day.
Will she wish to try it on?'

The professor turned to look at Jane, eyebrows
raised. 'It was a perfect fit, as I recall.' And when she
nodded speechlessly, he added, 'Wrap it up, if you
please, and be kind enough to let us see some winter
coats.'

Jane opened her mouth to protest and caught the
professor's eye. It had a steely glint and she decided
quite weakly to say nothing. There was no harm in
taking a look anyway.

A humbler version of the sales lady, hovering in the
background, was bidden to bring a selection of coats,
any one of which would have pleased the most
fashionable of young women. Jane took off the
raincoat and tried on the first of them, and, quite
carried away, tried on the rest in turn. The last one
of all took her fancy: a rich brown cashmere, cut
simply but with a swing to the skirt which suited her
Junoesque proportions.

The saleswoman was good at her job. 'An excellent
choice, if I might say so, madam; the colour comp-

lements your hair and the coat, being cashmere, is light and warm.' Her eyes swivelled to the professor, sitting on an elegant chair which creaked ominously under his weight, and he nodded.

Jane, examining her person from all angles, wondered about the price. Did one ask that in such a shop? Cashmere would be wildly expensive and did the professor realise that? There was really sure to be something less costly? Better still, from the point of view of his pocket, they need not buy a coat here at all, but go to Marks & Spencer at Marble Arch...

The professor's placid voice, begging her to keep the coat on, broke into her thoughts and, since she couldn't argue with him in front of the sales lady's sharp eyes, she did. Once outside on the pavement, she paused before getting into the car. 'Have you any idea how expensive cashmere is?' she asked him. 'I do hope it didn't cost too much. It's the loveliest coat I've ever had but I'm afraid it cost you too much... I could have bought a coat at Marks & Spencer...'

She looked quite beautiful staring up at him, her face framed by the soft brown collar. He bent and kissed her briefly, to the intense interest of the sales lady, who was peering from the shop window. 'Oh,' said Jane, taken by surprise but determined to finish what she had to say. 'And the dress—there was no need.'

He opened the car door and stuffed her carefully inside. 'Oh, but there was—you must wear it tomorrow evening when we go out to dinner.' As he closed the door he added, 'As for the coat, I can't have you catching cold and sniffing and snivelling your way up the aisle.'

She had to laugh then and he closed the door and got in beside her and drove on, back to Richmond, where he handed her over to Julie after the briefest of stays, dropping a careless kiss on Julie's cheek as he went and, much to Jane's disquiet, giving her a brotherly pat on the shoulder and nothing else. 'I'll call for you about eight o'clock,' was all he said, 'tomorrow.'

'I like that coat,' said Julie as they went into the sitting-room, 'and did you get the dress? Is that what is in the box?'

Jane nodded. 'Yes, it was a surprise. I'm not sure if I should...'

'You're going to marry Nik, aren't you?' observed Julie. 'Well, then, of course you may; besides, if he's taking you out tomorrow evening you'll need to dress up.' She patted the sofa beside her. 'Take off that lovely coat and come and sit down. When are you getting married?'

With a tray of coffee before them, the cats crammed between them and Bruno lying across their feet, this highly interesting subject was discussed at length.

'You'll need some clothes—not many, I should wait until you get to Holland and see what you need there. Nik has a great many friends; I dare say he'll want to take you about. All the same, you'll need something to be married in. Harrods, perhaps?'

Jane did some rather inaccurate arithmetic in her head. There was still a good deal of Granny's five hundred pounds in her bank account as well as the pittance Lady Grimstone had paid her. She nodded happily. 'Only tomorrow I must go back to Bessy and see about getting her a passport.'

'We'll take the car,' said Julie comfortably. 'Rex will know the quickest way to get to it, we'll ask him when he comes home. The passport office,' she added vaguely. 'He'll probably know someone who can see to it for you.'

Jane, warmly wrapped in the new coat, took the cats into the garden presently and then put on Bruno's lead and walked him briskly for an hour while she sorted out her muddled thoughts. A great deal seemed to have happened all at once and she had the feeling that she had rather lost control of her life, although she had to admit that there could be nothing nearer to her heart's desire than to allow the professor to control it for her.

'I shall marry him,' she told Bruno, trotting along beside her, 'and I shall make him happy—that is, I'll try and be exactly what he expects me to be.'

A good deal of the next day was taken up by dealing with Bessy and her passport. Appealed to, Rex smoothed their path, and the passport was promised in not later than ten days' time. That dealt with, Jane was able to bend her mind to the problem of clothes and she had whittled down her list to suitable proportions by the time the professor arrived that evening. This time he made a point of admiring the dress.

They went to the Savoy and danced and dined, their evening was wonderful and Jane loved every minute of it, quelling the faint disappointment at the professor's manner towards her—he could have been an older brother or a youthful uncle. She consoled herself with the fact that he enjoyed her company. They danced until the small hours and when he bade her goodnight he suggested that they might meet on the following day. 'Come to the hospital, will you? I should be free around one o'clock and I have no patients to see until three o'clock. We might have lunch together.'

She agreed quietly, anxious not to let him see how happy she was at the prospect of seeing him again so soon.

It was an opportunity to start looking for the small wardrobe she could afford; she saw to the cats and Bruno, and, waved away by a sympathetic Julie, took a bus to Regent Street where she prowled to and fro, pricing the clothes, trying to make up her mind which would be the best outfit to buy for the wedding. A prowl round Marks & Spencer decided her that a skirt, woollies and blouses from there would be in her best interest, a plain dress and undies, a warm dressing-gown and slippers; if she bought these there would be sufficient money over to splash out on something smart for her wedding—not too fashionable, she decided prudently, for she would have to wear it for the rest of the winter. The professor appeared to have plenty of money but she had no intention of spending it. She wasn't marrying him for that; she was marrying him because she loved him.

She was on her way to the hospital, taking a short cut through side-streets when she saw exactly what she had in mind: a dove-grey suit in soft wool with a blouse in the faintest of lavenders arranged beguilingly beside it. There was no time to go in and enquire as to its price; she would return the next day and buy it even if it meant drawing the last pound out of the bank.

She walked on air for the rest of the way and the professor, exchanging learned opinions with a colleague at the back of the entrance hall, watched her approach with an appreciative eye. She was a beautiful girl and a good companion; he had no doubt that they would make a success of their marriage. They liked each other, he reflected, and she was sensible and level-headed, happy to remain at home when he went on his frequent journeys to operate, consult or attend seminars. It would be a pleasure to come home to her.

Jane, unaware of his plans for her future, pushed open the swing doors, and he excused himself to his companion and went to meet her.

'Delightfully punctual,' he observed. 'I've booked a table at Le Poulbot.' He took her arm and walked across to where the Bentley was parked. As he got in beside her he said, 'I'll drive you back to Richmond after lunch—I should have liked to have taken you out again this evening but I must get some work done. I'm operating tomorrow but if I can get away I'll come to Julie's in the evening.' He smiled down at her. 'Have you had a pleasant morning? Did you do some shopping?'

'Well, not exactly shopping. I looked at things— I'll go again tomorrow now I've seen what I want.'

'Where would you like to be married?'

'If I could choose, at St Mary's, you know, the village at home, but of course that's not possible. There's a church near Julie's house—that would be convenient, wouldn't it?'

'Leave it to me. I've applied for a special licence so that we can marry where we wish.'

After that he had nothing more to say about their future. Jane, agog to know more about him—his family, his home, his friends—sensed that this wasn't

the time to ask. She was content just to be with him
and take part in the undemanding conversation he
started as they sat down to lunch. The restaurant was
one she had heard of but had never visited, the food
was French and delicious—lobster mousse, a tournedos with a red wine sauce and a coffee-flavoured *ba-
varoise* to finish. As she poured their coffee she said,
'That was lovely. You do know nice places to eat.'

'I have quite a few friends in London...'

She said slowly, 'Yes, I expect you have,' and then
she let her impetuous tongue get the better of her dis-
cretion. 'Didn't you want to marry? I mean... you
know what I mean.'

'Oh, I know what you mean, Jane. And in answer
to your unspoken question, I have taken charming
ladies out to dine and dance and enjoyed their
company, but I had no wish to marry. You see, none
of them would have put up with the kind of life I
could offer them for the simple reason that they were
totally uninterested in anything but amusing themselves and enjoying life—their kind of life.'

Jane said soberly, 'You don't know anything about
me. I might be just like that too.'

'Yes?' He raised his eyebrows. 'I cannot imagine
any one of them looking after her granny, putting up
with someone like Lady Grimstone, or traipsing round
England with two cats and a dog.' He smiled at her,
a nice reassuring smile. 'Have no fear, Jane, you are
exactly the wife I would wish for.'

'Well, as long as you're sure.'

Presently he drove her back to Richmond, bade her
a brief goodbye and took himself off with the re-
minder that he would see her on the next day.

Tomorrow, reflected Jane, watching the car slide away back towards London, I shall ask him a whole lot of questions.

She went back to take another look at the fine grey suit in the morning; it wasn't her size but the friendly woman who ran the shop was quite sure that she could get one in Jane's size. 'And the blouse too if you would like it?'

Jane, feeling reckless, agreed, and the woman said, 'Were you thinking of a hat? I've a rather special one that goes with the suit—it needs a hat, for it's what I call a special occasion outfit. A wedding, perhaps?' she said slyly.

'Well, yes, it is, and I do need a hat...'

It was a little velvet trifle the exact shade of the suit; it sat on her bright hair as though it had been specially created to do so and Jane bought it. A search through Oxford Street yielded shoes and gloves and there were still a few pounds left in her purse.

A good thing that Nik is so sure he wants to marry me, she thought, doing sums on the back of an envelope while she had a cup of tea, and, although she would have liked a bun to go with it, went without. Every penny counted.

It was several days later as she and Nik walked round Julie's quite large garden with Bruno, Percy and Simpkin that Jane was able to voice her thoughts. 'I know nothing about you,' she said with some asperity. 'Your parents—brothers and sisters, friends...'

He took her by the arm. 'My father died last year— he was a surgeon too, and a good one. My mother lives in Den Haag. Her family come from there and she didn't wish to stay at Vilerik—that is the village where my home is. She has a house between Den Haag

and the sea, near Wassenaar, which is a charming
suburb. I have two sisters, both married with children,
and innumerable aunts, uncles and cousins. I live
alone at Vilerik. Grimbert and Annis look after me
and Daisy my dog.'

'Oh, will she mind Bruno and the cats?'

'I think not. She is a gentle beast and will probably
be delighted to have company.'

They went indoors then for it was a cold evening
and there was no chance to talk any more. When he
went away she felt as though part of her had gone
with him and she was a little abstracted for the rest
of the evening. When Rex remarked upon it, Julie
said quickly, 'Jane's got a lot to think about—
clothes . . .' Rex laughed indulgently.

It wanted four days to the wedding, with Bessy's
passport and shopping dealt with, the grey suit
hanging in the wardrobe and Jane's rather shabby case
standing ready to be packed, when the professor arrived unexpectedly in the middle of the afternoon.
Julie had gone out and Jane was in the sitting-room,
kneeling before the fire, drying the hair she had just
washed. The noise of the door opening made her look
round.

Ethel beamed at her. 'It's the professor,' she explained, 'come to see you and, seeing you're as good
as wed, I'll show him in.'

Which she did. Jane parted her damp hair and
peered up at Nik as he crossed the room. Before she
could speak he said easily, 'Hello—don't get up. Give
me that towel and turn round.'

He sat down in a chair drawn up to the fire and
began to dry her hair. 'How pleasantly domestic,' he

observed, 'and what a striking head of hair you do have, Jane.'

She mumbled something and then said, 'I wasn't expecting you—Julie's out.'

'Good—we can have a talk.'

'What about?' Her heart lurched against her ribs; he had had second thoughts, the wedding was going to be postponed, his family didn't approve...

'I've fixed up our return to Holland on Saturday. Will you be ready by nine o'clock on Saturday morning? We'll drive down to St Mary's—the rector will marry us at half-past eleven.'

She shot round and stared at him. 'Nik—St Mary's... but it's so far and what about Basil?'

'Does he need to know? You wish to invite him? By all means if you like to do that, although I doubt if I'll be civil to him.'

'No. No, of course I don't want Basil, it's just that— oh, Nik, you've made me so happy, thank you over and over... But won't it be too much for you—all that way and then back to catch the ferry? And there's Bessy.'

He went on rubbing her beautiful head. 'No, it won't be too much for me.' He sounded as though he was laughing. 'And Bessy is to drive down with Rex and Julie and we shall all come back to my house for some kind of meal—we're going over on a hovercraft in the early evening; we should be at Vilerik by ten o'clock.'

'What about Bruno and the cats?'

'Slocombe will fetch them and they'll be waiting for us. You have all the necessary certificates?'

'Yes, yes, I have.' She had her back to him, her hair spread out over his knees as he dried it. 'Are you a bit scared, Nik?'

His voice was reassuringly placid. 'Not in the least. Are you?'

'Yes, just a bit. I keep thinking of the things that could go wrong.'

'It would be just as easy to think of all the things which could go right,' he observed with casual friendliness.

Julie came back presently and they all had tea round the fire, Jane with her hair tied back with a bit of ribbon and no make-up on her lovely face.

Saturday dawned, bride's weather: blue skies, and a thin winter sunshine to mitigate the wintry chill and a light frost to lend a sparkle to everything. Jane was up far too early, refusing to eat her breakfast in bed, getting into a skirt and pullover to take the three animals into the garden and then going to dress in the grey suit. She was waiting, a bundle of nerves, sitting upright in a chair in the drawing-room when the professor arrived, completely at his ease in a fine clerical dark grey suiting and a silk tie of a paler grey. At the sight of him Jane instantly felt at ease; everything was going to be all right; she loved him and she would love him forever and beyond. She gave him a wide smile and he bent to kiss her cheek. 'Ready?'

'Yes. I've seen to the cats and Bruno—Ethel will look after them until they're fetched. Bessy's here already.'

'You look exactly as a bride should look,' he told her. 'Quite beautiful.' He took a small doeskin bag from his pocket and unfastened it. 'Will you wear these?'

Pearls—a single strand, perfectly matched. 'Turn round,' he begged her, 'and I'll fasten them. I'll be very careful; I should hate to disarrange that hat.'

'They're beautiful,' said Jane, and went to peer at her reflection as Julie and Rex came into the room. 'We're just off,' said Rex. 'We'll see you at the church.'

'We'll leave in ten minutes,' Nik told her after they had gone, and strolled out into the garden while she went to say goodbye to Ethel and make sure that Bruno and the cats were safely with her.

It wasn't until they were almost there that Jane had the first twinges of panic. She had no doubt about herself, but what about the professor? Anything could happen to change his coolly planned future—he might meet someone and fall in love and what about the wedding? Supposing Basil had got to hear of it and was at the church and supposing Bessy wasn't happy in Holland?

The professor, looking sideways at her agitated-looking profile, said placidly, 'If you don't stop worrying this very minute, you will look at least forty years old. Nothing awful is going to happen; indeed I have the firm conviction that we shall find marriage very much to our liking.'

'Do you really? You see, it's not quite like the usual marriage, is it?'

'As to that, ask me again in a few months' time. Here we are.' He laid a hand briefly on her knee. 'You look beautiful, Jane; remember that as you go up the aisle.'

Mr Chepstow was waiting in the porch to give her away and before the professor left them there he gave her a small bouquet—pink roses, lily of the valley and, here and there, forget-me-nots. He patted her on a shoulder as he did so in an encouraging manner and Jane wished that he had kissed her instead.

She was surprised to hear the organ being played, she hadn't expected that nor, when they opened the inner door and started down the aisle of the little church, had she expected to see so many people in it. No sign of Basil, however, she noted with relief.

Everyone she had known in the village was there, smiling at her as she went to meet the professor, who was standing with Rex beside him, and turned to look at her as she reached his side.

Presently she was walking out of the church again, this time with her hand on Nik's arm, smiling at everyone. It was like being in a dream, she reflected as people she had known for years crowded round them, wishing them well.

There wasn't much time to do more than greet everyone, Nik popped her back into the car after bidding the rector goodbye and they drove away from the group of well-wishers.

'How kind of everyone to come to our wedding,' said Jane happily. 'What a pity we couldn't have stayed—beer and sandwiches and things,' she added vaguely.

'It's open house at the pub for anyone who likes to go,' said Nik cheerfully.

'You arranged that? Thank you, Nik—you think of everything. I was so relieved not to see Basil...'

'The village was sworn to secrecy but you can be sure that he'll hear about it before the day is over.'

'You've been to a lot of trouble—thank you very much.' She felt suddenly shy of him and sat twiddling her wedding-ring round and round her finger. Without looking at him she said, 'I can't quite believe that we're married.' She went on 'Mrs van der Vollenhove...'

'Barones van der Vollenhove,' and when she turned to look at him in astonishment, 'I'm Jonkheer van der Vollenhove, but over here we're just Mr and Mrs.'

She said faintly, 'Oh, are we? You didn't tell me.'

He said easily, 'Oh, it rather slipped my mind,' which was such palpable nonsense that she laughed.

She enjoyed the drive back to London. They would get on well, she told herself; they liked each other and she loved him, and, full of the morning's euphoria, she could see no reason why, in the course of time, he shouldn't fall in love with her too.

At his house Slocombe was waiting with dignified congratulations and a splendid buffet lunch, and as soon as Rex and Julie and Bessy arrived he handed the smoked salmon, quails' eggs, anchovy toasts and miniature quiches, while the professor opened the champagne.

They didn't linger; they had a hovercraft to catch. Bessy was fetched from the meal she had enjoyed with Slocombe, the animals were stowed in the back of the car beside her, and Jane bade goodbye to Julie and Rex and got back into the car. Nothing seemed quite real, what with the champagne and the excitement of it all; she sat silently as the professor drove away with a casual wave to Slocombe. The professor was silent too but presently he spoke to Bessy over his shoulder and started a desultory conversation about nothing much as they drove to Dover.

It was early evening and dark by the time they landed, and once they were clear of the town and joined the motorway there was nothing to see. Bessy, with Bruno on her lap, had gone to sleep, and Percy and Simpkin were silent. Jane was silent too, her eyes on the professor's large well kept hands on the wheel, but presently she asked, 'Do you always come this way?'

'Not always—but at this time of year and at the end of the day the roads are good and fast; we shall be home in less than two hours.'

It seemed no time at all before he said quietly, 'Here's the border...'

He picked up speed again, the road stretching almost empty before them, the lights from towns and villages easily seen in the flat country around them. He slowed again as they took the ring-road round Utrecht and, still on the motorway, drove north towards Amsterdam, but presently the professor took a turn-off and then a narrow brick road. There were no lights and the dark was profound but Jane caught a gleam of water presently and then, ahead of them, twinkling lights. 'Vilerik,' said Nik, and at the same time slowed the car to go through the narrow main street of the small village, turn sharply into a lane beside the church and drive between high brick pillars. The drive was short and curved and Jane could see the lighted windows from the house at its end. There seemed to be a great many of them, and she said so with a touch of uneasiness.

The professor ignored her, stopped silently before his front door and got out. As he opened her door he took her arm. 'Welcome to your home, my dear,' he said quietly, and turned away to help Bessy out.

The door had been opened, letting out a stream of light, and a portly man came down the front steps. He greeted the professor with a beaming smile, shook the hand Jane offered and, since it was obvious that Bessy's hand was to be shaken too, she put her own out awkwardly with a, 'How do you do?' uttered uncertainly, giving a sigh of relief when he said,

'I do well, Miss Bessy; my name is Grimbert.'

The door opened on to a glass lobby and that in turn opened into a square hall, panelled and hung with oil-paintings, the floor black and white marble, the furniture, a console table and some armchairs, old and polished.

Jane had no time to look around her. 'The cats had better go for a quick stroll,' said the professor in a matter-of-fact voice. 'Grimbert can see to the luggage and show Bessy where to go while we take these three for a walk.'

The cats were cross, naturally enough, but Bruno was delighted to be with Jane again. The professor opened his front door once more and led the little party outside into the cold evening, picking up a small rug in the lobby as they went and putting it around Jane's shoulders.

'And what about your coat?' said Jane.

He took her arm. 'You sound exactly like a wife,' he observed, laughing.

The animals had no wish to linger. They all went back to the comforting warmth of the hall where Grimbert was waiting to take the rug.

'I expect you'd like to feed these three before anything else?' said the professor. 'Grimbert will take you to the kitchen and see to it—on second thoughts I'd better come too in case Daisy gets flustered.'

'Daisy?'

'My dog, remember? A golden labrador and most amiable.'

He led her through a baize door, along a short stone-flagged passage and into the kitchen, a large square room with great dressers on its walls and an Aga taking up one end, flanked by glass-fronted cupboards. The table in its centre was square too and well scrubbed with high-backed wooden chairs drawn up to it.

Grimbert wasn't there, but his wife was, a tall bony woman with a long face and grey hair severely drawn back from it; she looked up and smiled as they went in and came over to shake hands with the professor and Jane while Daisy capered around, delighted to see her master again. There was another woman in the room, much younger, with a round cheerful face and already buxom. She came to shake hands too and the professor said, 'This is Grimbert's wife and my housekeeper—Annis—and this is the housemaid, Bep, and this, of course, is Daisy.'

Daisy was sitting by them panting happily while Bruno made friends and Percy and Simpkin explored the kitchen, aware, no doubt, that Daisy was a friend. Food was produced, saucers and bowls arranged tidily in one corner, and the animals fed before they all went back into the hall again.

'Come in here,' invited Nik, opening a door and pausing to say, 'Of course, this is all the wrong way to do it, isn't it? I should have carried you over the threshold, shouldn't I, and taken you straight into a flower-filled room and given you champagne? Instead of which we feed the cats in the kitchen.'

Perhaps that was to set the pattern of their lives together, reflected Jane, being sensible and leaving the flowers and champagne for those in love. She conjured up a plausible laugh. 'I'm no sylph; you might have dropped me, and besides the animals needed their supper, didn't they?'

She went past him into the room. 'And this is even better than flowers and champagne—what a delightful room.'

They stood together in the centre of the room and he flung an arm around her shoulders in a friendly fashion. 'The small sitting-room—I use it a great deal when I'm not in the study. There is a drawing-room but it's rather vast—we save it for special occasions.'

It was indeed a charming place with long wide windows facing the back of the house, draped in amber velvet. The floor was polished wood, covered with rugs patterned in vague greens and blues. Bow-fronted cabinets housed china and silver along its walls and there were easy-chairs and a vast sofa drawn up to the brisk fire in the marble fireplace. Lamps with amber-coloured shades stood on the small piecrust tables and overhead was an antique brass chandelier, throwing light on to the numerous paintings on the walls. Jane took it all in, wondering what a large sitting-room would be like if this was the small one, although she didn't say so. She sensed that Nik had grown up with the room and its treasures and took it for granted.

'Sit down and have a drink. Grimbert will be in presently to tell us supper is ready.'

Jane sat down. 'What about Bessy?'

'Grimbert will take care of her. They'll have supper together and get to know each other. We'll go and see her presently.'

He took her across the hall to the dining-room, larger than the sitting-room and furnished massively, with a rectangular mahogany table, ringed by a dozen chairs, a vast sideboard and a long silver-table, beautifully carved and with a serpentine front, against one wall.

Here they had their supper—soup, a ragout of chicken and chocolate custards piled high with cream, and by the time they had eaten these Jane was sleepy. Grimbert served their coffee at the table and presently Nik said kindly, 'You're tired after such a long day, Jane; Annis shall take you to your room and you can say goodnight to Bessy on the way.'

'Aren't you tired too?' she said.

'I have some work to do,' he told her, smiling, and went to open the door for her. She wished him goodnight and looked up at him as she went past, expecting his kiss, but he smiled and touched her gently on the shoulder. 'Sleep well—breakfast is at eight o'clock but have it in bed if you would like that.'

For all the world as if we had been married for half a lifetime, she thought unhappily as she followed Annis upstairs, but, after all, it was only what she had expected, wasn't it?

CHAPTER EIGHT

THE staircase was rather grand, sweeping up one side of the hall in a graceful curve to the gallery above. Annis turned to the left at the head of the stairs, opened a heavy mahogany door and ushered Jane into the room. It was at the front of the house with a door, flanked by two windows, opening on to a covered balcony. Annis went to draw the old rose brocade curtains and turn on more lights, and Jane took a quick look around her. The four-poster was of maple wood and hung with matching brocade, and the dressing-table was of the same wood, carved and inlaid with a Dutch marquetry mirror. A giltwood Regency day bed stood at the foot of the bed and two velvet-covered armchairs flanked a Pembroke table. Annis, drawing her attention to the door leading to the bathroom and another opening into a clothes closet of enormous size, interrupted her inspection.

She smiled at Annis, who smiled back encouragingly. 'Bessy?'

Annis's smile widened and she led the way out of the room to the back of the gallery and up another staircase, knocked on the door of the end room, nodded cheerfully and went away.

Bessy's voice, surprisingly cheerful, bade her go in and Jane opened the door. Bessy was bending over her case, unpacking, but she turned round when Jane went in.

'Miss Jane, I don't know if I'm on me 'ead or me 'eels, that I don't. It's a palace, and everyone so nice. That Grimbert and 'is wife, as nice a pair as I ever set eyes on, we 'ad a good laugh over our supper, and look at this room.' She beamed at Jane. 'Just you sit down for a minute and tell me you're the 'appiest girl in the world . . .'

Since it was expected of her, Jane did just that, adding, 'And tomorrow we'll go over the house properly and I dare say Grimbert will explain any jobs you're to do . . .'

Bessy nodded. 'The ironing—Annis don't like ironing and the master's that fussy about 'is shirts, and 'elping with the silver and the beds—I 'aven't been so 'appy for a long time, Miss Jane, and you're 'appy too?' She chuckled, 'And Bruno and Simpkin and Percy, sitting around as if to the manner born. I just wish your granny could see us now, though, like as not, she can.'

Jane bade her an affectionate goodnight and went back to her room. Someone had unpacked her cases and her nightie was lying on the bed, but before she got ready for bed she opened the doors on to the balcony and went outside. It was piercingly cold now but there were still lights streaming from the downstairs windows and as she looked the front door was opened and the professor, with the two dogs and Percy and Simpkin on their leads, came out and went down the steps and on to the wide sweep of lawn; he looked up as he crossed the gravel of the drive and he must have seen her though he gave no sign, and in a moment she went in, closed the doors and pulled the curtains across. She wanted very much to be with him, pacing the grass together in the cold night, but he hadn't wanted her.

She undressed slowly and after a long, hot bath got into the four-poster bed. It was the acme of comfort and she should have slept at once, but she didn't, she was still awake, too tired to think but her head full of Nik, when she heard his steady tread across the gallery on his way to bed.

When she woke in the morning the night's fears and worries had evaporated. She dressed and went downstairs and found Nik already at the table, the animals sitting side by side before the fire, Grimbert trotting to and fro with coffee and tea and fresh toast.

The professor got up from his chair, bade her good morning, hoped that she had slept well and asked her if she would like to go to church with him. 'The village church,' he explained. 'The service isn't so very different from your church...'

'I'd like to go. At what time...?'

'Ten o'clock; plenty of time to stroll round the grounds first and a chance for the animals to explore.'

She agreed happily, ate her breakfast quickly and went to fetch her coat. They went out of a small side-door and this time the cats went free and, though Jane was nervous of them running off, they did no such thing but stayed fairly close while Daisy and Bruno raced around on their own.

The grounds were spacious and walled and they spent a pleasant half-hour before going back into the house where Jane went in search of Bessy, whom she found in the kitchen, sitting at the table, rubbing up the table silver.

'There you are, Miss Jane,' she exclaimed happily. 'My goodness, 'ave I fallen on me feet—I can't believe me own eyes and everyone so kind—the professor popped in to see me too, wanted to know if I 'ad everything I needed. There's a gentleman for yer, as I told Mr Grimbert. You don't never 'ave ter worry about me for the rest of me days, Miss Jane, dear, for I'm that 'appy.'

Jane had gone to sit by her. 'Oh, Bessy, I'm so glad. All the same, if you have any worries you're to tell me at once . . .'

'Me? I'll 'ave no worries from now on, and you neither, Miss Jane.'

Jane got into the car presently beside the professor and was driven the short distance to the village. The church was almost full and she was conscious of being stared at, not unkindly but in a speculative fashion, but Nik's reassuring bulk beside her in the high pew gave her confidence and after the service, which, despite the lengthy and thunderous sermon, wasn't so very unlike her own church, she responded with friendly dignity to the numerous introductions Nik made. The *dominee*, who had thundered fire and brimstone from the pulpit, turned out to be a mild man who spoke excellent English with a wife who was just as mild. Her smattering of English was adequate and Jane had no doubt that they would like each other.

There were other people to meet too, local dignitaries she supposed, who eyed her cautiously while being polite, addressing her in sparse English.

'You will see a good deal of the local people,' Nik told her as they drove back to Vilerik House. 'I have little time to be social but now that I am married they will call, invite us to dine and drink coffee. You will be a great help to me if you will accept the invitations where my absence won't matter.' And when she looked at him enquiringly, 'I am away all day and frequently I need to go to one or other hospital in the evening, so you must deputise for me at the various coffee mornings and tea parties which everyone is bound to organise.'

'Am I to return these invitations?'

'Of course—during the day when I'm not at home. I treasure my evenings when I'm free, Jane. There is a certain social life attached to the hospitals too— official dinners and receptions, that kind of thing, to which we will go together.' He drew up before his front door and turned to look at her. 'I have friends too— close friends. Now that we are married, they will come and spend weekends from time to time.'

Jane went into the house with him, reflecting that there would be no fear of having too little to do as his wife. Not his wife really, she conceded, more like a personal assistant or a trusty right hand to be thoroughly relied upon. All the same, she would do her best; she loved him too much to contemplate anything else.

It was surprising how quickly she slipped into the pattern of the days; Christmas was almost upon them and they were to spend it at Den Haag—a family gathering, Nik had told her, when she would meet everyone. In the meantime he spent his days at the hospitals where he had beds, operating and seeing patients. Since his day began early, she breakfasted with him before eight o'clock each morning, sitting opposite him quietly while he skimmed through his post. Her days were full enough; the dogs to walk, the cats to see to, Bessy to chat with, various small household duties, walks to the village to meet the *dominee* to discuss flowers for the church, sweets for the Sunday school children at Christmas. She kept herself busy until Nik returned home each evening to find her waiting for him, sitting in the charming room by the fire with the animals lounging around her, busy with the wool and needles she had prudently purchased in the village shop. She had asked no questions of him, made no mention of her lack of a suitable wardrobe, not uttered a grumbling word about his total absorption in his work...

She was rewarded for this at the end of the week. Sitting opposite her, sipping the whisky she had ready for him, watching her quietly knitting, the lamplight casting a rosy glow over her head, he said suddenly, 'I've neglected you shamefully, Jane. I am so used to coming back here and getting straight down to work that I quite forgot that I am a married man. I'm free tomorrow; we'll go shopping if you would like that—clothes for Christmas—presents...' He put a gentle hand on Daisy's head. 'Can you buy all you want in one day, do you suppose?'

'Well, it's according to what I have to buy. If you give me a list of the people who are to have presents then I'll do my best.'

'Good. And you? You will need dresses and so on? We will go directly after breakfast.'

The day had been absolute bliss, decided Jane, curled up in bed the following night. Over an early breakfast they had discussed the list of presents to be bought and she had been invited to make a list for herself. 'Warm clothes,' the professor had advised her, 'and party dresses, a short leather jacket, something suitable for the visits I make to the hospitals on Christmas Day...' The list had grown to outrageous proportions, but when she had attempted to pare it down he had told her to leave it as it was.

The presents had been dealt with with ease and speed; what a difference it made, reflected Jane, when there was no need to look at the price tags; pure silk scarves for his sisters, a handbag for his mother, a thick crimson dressing-gown for Bessy, gloves and slippers, toys for nieces and nephews...

That was only the beginning; before they'd had their lunch she had found herself the possessor of a suede jacket, tweed skirts—Burberry, she'd noted—an elegant suit in dark green, a cashmere shirt-dress and a couple of patterned jersey dresses. After lunch she had been walked smartly to an elegant arcade of boutiques and jewellers where she acquired a cream taffeta ballgown, three short dresses which Nik had assured her would be just the thing for parties, a handful of blouses and several fine wool sweaters. And as if this weren't enough, he had taken her to the Maison de Bonneterie and told her to buy all the undies she liked. 'I'll meet you here in half an hour,' he told her.

'I haven't any money,' she told him breathlessly. 'This looks a very expensive shop and you've spent a fortune this morning. Isn't there somewhere cheaper?'

He shook his head, smiling down at her. 'Buy anything you like,' he told her again. 'Mention my name and tell them to put everything on the bill.'

So she had done just that, choosing cautiously at first, and then, carried away by the lovely gossamer things on display, quite recklessly.

He had been there in half an hour, waiting patiently until she had finished and then signing a cheque without a quiver before loading her parcels into the car and taking her to tea at a smart very expensive café in Lange Vooruit.

It had been a pity that he had gone to his study when they got back, telling her that he would see her at dinner; on the other hand, she told herself reasonably, it had given her the chance to show everything to Bessy and give that faithful friend the dress she and Nik had chosen together. Afterwards she had put on one of the new dresses and gone down to the sitting-room. There had still been no sign of Nik, so she had put on her raincoat, collected up the dogs and cats and gone out into the garden. It had been cold with a pale moon and frost already crackling under her feet. They hadn't stayed out long and when they had gone inside again Nik was there—he had admired the new dress too. She went to sleep now, happy about that.

She woke in the small hours, engulfed by a tearing grief, knowing without any doubt that loving Nik wasn't going to be enough, and how could she have been such a fool as to believe that? Her love had let her be blinded to the fact that all he wanted was companionship; an easygoing partnership which wouldn't interfere with his work and would smooth his path through the various calls upon his social life. That he was fond of her she had no doubt, but that was all— and that wasn't enough . . .

She gulped back tears and sat up in bed. It was a state of affairs which needed to be put right and the fact that she was the one to do it stuck out like a sore thumb. Not a conceited girl, she was nevertheless aware that she was blessed with a lovely face, an arresting head of hair and a splendid figure; obviously these alone weren't enough to arouse the professor's deeper interest. Partly her own fault, for she had never made any bid to attract him; indeed, on several occasions she had wept all over his shirt-front, besides running away from him in the most ungrateful manner. The unpleasant thought that perhaps he was nurturing a secret passion for some unattainable female and was making do with second-best—namely herself—merely served to increase her determination to do something and do it without delay. She must attract his attention . . .

There had been an invitation to have coffee with the *dominee* and his wife and Nik had agreed casually that she should go. 'A splendid idea,' he had said. 'I dare say you'll meet quite a few people—you met some of them last Sunday. We must give a drinks party at New Year—the family, friends and so on . . .'

She was a nice girl with a kind heart but a little ruthlessness might be a good idea . . . make him jealous? Do something to lift her out of the calm background in which he seemed content to leave her?

Her mind made up, Jane curled up and went to sleep again.

It seemed that kindly providence was going to lend a hand; the *dominee's* wife had invited a number of people to meet her, all of whom knew the professor and were only too delighted to welcome her as his wife. Better still, Mevrouw van der Blom, who lived on the other side of the village, had her brother staying with her, a handsome, rather rakish type. Jane lost no time in inviting them for drinks. She asked several others too but she smiled enchantingly at him . . .

She waited until Nik was sitting opposite her at the dinner-table that evening before she mentioned her invitations. 'I know it will annoy you,' she observed in a meek voice which made him look at her thoughtfully, 'but they seemed to expect it. Only eight people...' She recited their names. 'Oh, and Mevrouw van der Blom had a brother staying with her—she asked if he might come too,' she added, 'tomorrow.'

She gave him a guileless look from her green eyes. 'They asked us to dinner but I said you couldn't possibly go as you would be working.'

The professor kept his eyes on her face. She looked beautiful and as innocent as a child. He wondered what she was up to and felt a faint stirring of disquiet followed by amusement. Probably she was eager to get to know everyone as quickly as possible. He said, 'Quite right, I've a good deal of work to get through before Christmas but by all means have people in for drinks. The director of the hospital at Hilversum is giving a reception next week—we must go, of course. I think you may enjoy it.'

'Will you be free over Christmas?'

'After lunch on Christmas Eve and hopefully until the day after the second Christmas Day. We shall be in Den Haag on the first Christmas Day, of course.'

'Yes. Nik, what do I wear to this reception?'

He gave her a kind smile. 'Drinks from six o'clock until eight—a short dress—you will need to wear that ballgown in the New Year for the ball in Amsterdam.'

She nodded. 'The *dominee's* wife asked me if I would help with the Sunday school party—it's in the afternoon. I said that I would...'

'Splendid.' They had finished dinner and were walking across to the sitting-room for their coffee, as he asked, 'You're happy, Jane?'

Her, 'Oh, yes,' was so emphatic that he felt disquiet for the second time that evening.

She dressed with care the following evening in one of the patterned jersey dresses; its green matched her eyes exactly and save for the pearls and her engagement and wedding-rings she wore no jewellery. With her hair wound in a chignon and her feet in new high-heeled shoes, she studied her reflection and felt satisfied. She wore rather more make-up than usual too, a fact which Bessy, coming upon her as she went down to the drawing-room, noticed.

'Lawks, Miss Jane, you've got yerself up and no mistake—not that you don't look smashing...'

'Why, thank you, Bessy.' Jane beamed at her and changed her mind about going into the drawing-room for the moment. The sitting-room was cosy and the two cats and two dogs, sprawling in an untidy heap before the fire, made the handsome room very homelike. They didn't stir when she went in, although they eyed her, and presently she went back to the drawing-room. She wasn't quite used to its grandeur yet, though she had explored it thoroughly several times. She and Nik hadn't sat in it together but it seemed fitting that it should be used this evening— with ten or so people in it it might not seem so vast or so grand. There was a fire burning in its hooded grate and the soft lighting shone on the brocades of the chairs and the polished tables and cabinets.

She was sitting there when the professor came home. He paused in the doorway to look at her and, since she had taken care to sit with the rosy glow of a table lamp casting just the right amount of light and shade upon her person, she was worth looking at. She got to her feet with a show of surprise and went to meet him. 'Nik—how nice, you're early. Grimbert has put out the drinks but I'm glad you're here to make sure they're all right.'

He smiled down at her. 'That's a pretty dress. Give me fifteen minutes.'

He was coming down the staircase as the first of the guests arrived so that they were there to meet them together and Jane, concealing shyness behind her calm face, was glad of his reassuring company.

Mevrouw van der Blom, with her husband and brother at her heels, came last. Jane, circulating politely, found him beside her presently; indeed he remained close to her during the next hour or so, engaging her in small talk, looking at her with open admiration. Jane, aware of Nik's glance from time to time, behaved circumspectly without discouraging her admirer, but when he suggested that he might call one afternoon and take her for a drive she declined with what she hoped was matronly dignity. 'But it's very kind of you to ask me,' she added, and smiled with sweetness at him because Nik was watching from the other end of the room, then turned away to talk to the *dominee's* wife.

'A very pleasant evening,' observed the professor evenly as they sat at the dinner-table later. 'I can see that I may safely leave the social side of our life in your capable hands.'

Jane cast down her eyes so that her lashes swept her cheeks. 'Why, Nik, thank you, but there won't be any more unless you say so. I know you like to spend your evenings quietly.' Butter wouldn't have melted in her mouth.

'Corrie van der Blom's brother—Wilber—seemed very taken with you.'

Jane composed her features into childlike innocence. 'Oh, no—he was practising his English. He was very kind, though—he offered to show me something of the country around here but I said no of course—there's the Sunday school party and the presents to wrap up and I want to do some shopping.' She smiled at him across the table. 'Is there a car I could borrow? I saw Grimbert driving to Amsterdam this morning in a little Fiat...'

The professor sat back in his chair. 'Of course you can have a car. You have your licence with you? You feel quite at ease about driving on the other side of the road? You can understand the road signs?'

'Well, no, but will there be any on the motorway?'

'Where did you propose to go?' he asked with interest.

'Well, Hilversum is quite near, isn't it? I want to buy a dictionary and a Dutch grammar and pens and a notebook.' She swept her eyelashes up with devastating effect. At least she hoped it was devastating; she had practised long enough in front of the looking-glass in her room...

'I'm going to Hilversum tomorrow morning directly after breakfast. I'll give you a lift. I've a clinic there and should be free around noon—I'll show you where to meet me.'

'But you never come home for lunch.'

She had spoken without thinking and wished that she hadn't, for he gave her a little mocking smile although his eyes were cold. Refusing to be intimidated, she went on, 'Well, only on Sunday and when we went to Den Haag.'

'I must change my habits, must I not?'

She remembered all her good resolutions. 'Only if you want to,' she told him airily. 'I dare say it is a great waste of time coming home during the day.'

His chilly stare was making her feel uncomfortable and she plunged into speech. 'Mevrouw ten Crocq—she told me that she had known you a long time—asked if we could go to dinner one evening. I said that you wouldn't be free until the New Year—I hope that was the right thing to say? I'm going there for coffee—you don't mind?'

He was casual. 'Certainly not—she is a very old family friend. Who else will be there?'

'She said several people who knew you and your family.' Then she added airily, 'Wilber is calling for me with his car.'

'Very civil of him,' commented the professor suavely. 'Shall we go back to the drawing-room? It seems a pity to waste that splendid fire there.'

Thinking about it later, Jane wondered if she had had any success with her scheme. Certainly she had annoyed him and perhaps that was a good sign.

Hilversum looked very modern but its streets were wide and the shops she glimpsed as they went through the town looked promising. Nik drew up before the hospital gates and got out to open her door. 'Go down that narrow street.' He pointed out a lane beside the hospital. 'The main street is just at its end. Shall you be ready by noon? If I'm not already here come into the hospital, say who you are, and wait.'

He took her arm and saw her to the lane. 'Enough money?' he asked as they parted.

'More than enough, Nik.' The roll of notes she had found beside her plate at breakfast—her monthly allowance, he had told her—was more than generous.

She spent a delightful morning, browsing in a vast book shop, buying the books the bookseller advised her to and then, after coffee in a chic café, window shopping. There was really nothing she wanted, although she felt compelled to buy a long black velvet evening skirt and the pale peach chiffon blouse which went with it.

There was no sign of Nik when she reached the hospital, so she went through its massive doors and addressed herself to the man in the porter's lodge. 'Professor van der Vollenhove?' she enquired of the solid man sitting in his little booth.

He smiled then and, to her surprise, shook her hand, came out of his cubbyhole and led her to the back of the large hall to where there were a number of desks with a young woman behind each of them.

He spoke to the first of them and she shook hands too with the observation in English that she was delighted to meet the wife of the professor, whom she was to escort to the surgical wing. 'For he has been a little delayed,' she explained as she ushered Jane into a lift.

The surgical wing like the rest of the hospital was modern and up-to-date with its equipment. Jane, following her guide, peered from side to side as she went and wished she had had more time to look at her leisure, but they fetched up before double doors and just the other side of those was a corridor with a ward at its end and a great many doors on either side.

Her guide tapped on the first one, opened it, wished her goodbye and hurried away, leaving Jane to go in. It was quite a large room and seemed full of people,

partly, she supposed, because the professor and the
two younger men with him were all large. The ward
sister behind the desk was a big woman too; she got
up as Jane hesitated at the door but it was the professor who took her arm and led her forward.

'Hello, my dear.' He spoke in English. 'Come and
meet my colleagues. Hoofdzuster Spijk, Cor van Dijk,
my registrar and Henk Eysink, the surgical officer.'

She shook hands all round, murmured suitably and
smiled charmingly, aware that she was looking her
best, exchanging small talk with Zuster Spijk; yes, she
found Holland quite delightful and yes, she would be
coming to the reception and she was looking forward
to meeting her husband's friends, but presently she
found herself with the two men while Nik discussed
something with Zuster Spijk and she was pleasantly
aware that they were attracted to her and, what was
more to the point, Nik was aware of it too. She made
her farewells gracefully and accompanied him down
to the car and as they drove away remarked how
pleased she had been to get a glimpse of a Dutch hospital. He made some non-committal reply so presently she said chattily, 'I bought something—the shops
are rather splendid here, aren't they?' and, since he
gave a grunt in reply, 'Do you have time to go anywhere else today?' and, not giving him time to answer,
'Grimbert is going to get out the Fiat this afternoon;
he said he'll come with me until I get used to the
driving. You don't mind?'

'Why should I mind, Jane? I have to go to Utrecht
after lunch and shall probably be back about seven
o'clock.'

There was nothing in his face to tell her that he was
in fact free for the rest of the day, with a half-formed
idea of spending it alone with her. He had been so

sure that their marriage was a sensible arrangement between two people who liked each other, and he did like Jane although he had had no intention of letting her alter his life and she had understood that, but now after only a few weeks he found himself thinking too much about her. He frowned. He had always thought her beautiful; it was apparent that other men did too although she had behaved beautifully and with cool dignity. He stopped the car before the house and got out to help her with her parcels. It was strange, he mused, that he hadn't considered that when he proposed marriage to her. He had been quite certain that he had wanted to marry her but now he admitted that perhaps he had overlooked one possibility, that of falling in love with her. Ridiculous, of course; he hadn't fallen in love for years and had never had to feel a lasting hurt; his work engrossed him and he had long ago decided that he would make that the important thing in his life.

They went indoors together to have lunch and presently to take the dogs and cats for a walk around the grounds before Jane, businesslike in her new quilted jacket and sensible shoes, got into the car beside Grimbert. Nik, who had left shortly before, had gone in the direction of Utrecht but she, obedient to her companion, took the quiet road which encircled the nearby lake of Loenen and then back on to the Hilversum road and so finally on to the Amsterdam motorway which, to her relief, wasn't as frightening as she had expected. She was back in time for tea, rather pleased with herself and Grimbert's dignified praise.

Long before seven o'clock she was downstairs again, dressed in the new skirt and chiffon blouse, and when she heard the car she nipped smartly up the staircase until she heard the key in the lock before beginning a slow descent, to stop with a most realistic start of surprise as Nik came into the hall. It had been worth a little thought—the great chandelier unlit, only the wall sconces with their pink shades to cast a gentle glow, thinking out the best spot on which to pause so that from his viewpoint she would look her very best... She tripped down the last few treads and crossed the hall to where he stood.

'Oh, very nice, Jane.' There was a hint of laughter in his voice and she knew that he had seen through her small subterfuge, but she chose to ignore that. She gave him a smiling look.

'You like it? I bought it this morning.' She twirled round on her high-heeled slippers.

'More guests?' His tone was dry as he switched on the chandelier lights, destroying the pink-tinted romantic dimness.

'No, no. I would have told you. The New Year, you said—when you have more time. The *dominee's* wife—and I suppose it's the same as the Mothers' Union—are coming to tea tomorrow—fifteen of them. You don't mind?'

He had taken off his coat and was leaning against a console table, his hands in his pockets. 'Ah, yes—I believe my mother started something like that; an excellent idea. And as for guests, I can promise you a busy time once Christmas is over—all three hospitals have plans for receptions and dances and you have yet to meet my friends.'

'Have you had a busy afternoon?'

He had spent it, not in Utrecht, but away from that city, driving into the wooded region to the east of it until he reached Treek-Henschoten, a vast area where one might walk for miles. He had left the car and done just that, striding along in a biting wind, acknowledging at last and to his own surprise that he was falling in love with Jane—and what was to be done about it? He had reached no conclusion by the time he had reached his home but the sight of her in her pretty clothes, standing on the staircase as he went into the house, had merely served to strengthen his feelings. He said now, 'Yes. Give me ten minutes and I'll join you in the sitting-room.'

He went upstairs, Daisy at his heels, and she went to sit by the fire with the cats at her feet and Bruno pressed against her skirt. She had surprised him, she reflected with satisfaction, and that was a start.

It was disappointing that after a pleasant dinner together he should plead urgent paperwork waiting for him in the study.

Bessy, coming to collect the coffee-tray later, paused to say, 'On yer own, Miss Jane? An' in such a pretty outfit too.' She picked up the tray and put it down again. 'You're 'appy, aren't you? 'E's a good 'usband, isn't 'e? You love 'im?'

'I love him very much, Bessy. And you, Bessy, are you happy here?'

'Lor' bless yer, Miss Jane, it's 'eaven.' She waited a minute but Jane said nothing, only smiled, and she picked up the tray again.

Later Jane took herself off to bed, going first to the study and opening the door to peer round it. The professor, doing nothing behind his desk, got up. 'Jane . . .'

She didn't give him the chance to say more. 'Don't stop your work,' she begged him kindly. 'Goodnight, Nik.'

When she went down to breakfast in the morning, he was on the point of leaving the house. 'There's an emergency at Amsterdam. I dare say I'll be operating some time today. If anyone phones, tell them to ring there, will you?'

She ate her breakfast quickly, attended to the animals' various needs, took the dogs for a walk and asked Grimbert to get the Fiat out of the garage for her. A trip to Amsterdam would be fun; besides, she had to find a present for Nik.

She didn't much enjoy the drive to the city but she found a place to park and, as good luck would have it, found the present too. A small bronze statue of a child, small enough to have a place on his desk. She bore it back to the car and, pleased with herself, started to drive back home.

She hadn't been driving for more than a minute or two when she realised that she had taken a wrong turning. There was a lot of traffic and it seemed prudent to go on and hope for the best. Five minutes later she pulled into the side of the street; she would have to ask the way but the cars behind her blew their horns in a frenzy of impatience so she drove on.

Into a one-way street running past the main city hospital.

The professor, standing at a window of the theatre unit waiting to scrub, had a splendid view of the street below. He watched with interest as the small car, going the wrong way, wove its way carefully against the indignant oncoming traffic. He had excellent eyesight and he recognised the Fiat easily enough and when Jane put her arm out to signal that she would turn left, since it seemed the best thing to do, he recognised the brown coat sleeve.

'Oh, God,' said the professor, who was a God-fearing man, and reached for the phone.

CHAPTER NINE

JANE, doggedly pursuing her way in the hope of finding it eventually, was startled when a traffic policeman on a scooter came alongside her and waved her to a halt. She edged into the kerb and stuck her head out of the window. 'I hope you can speak English?'

'Yes, *mevrouw*, enough. You are lost?'

'Yes, how did you know? Oh, of course, someone must have told you that I went down a one-way street. So sorry.' She smiled at him. 'This is only the second time I have driven in Holland. It's a bit confusing. Do you want to fine me?'

The policeman was a beefy, middle-aged man, rather solemn. 'No, *mevrouw*. If you will follow me I will show you the best way out of the city.'

'That's very kind of you. I want to go to a village called Vilerik ...'

He nodded. 'Follow me, *mevrouw*.'

The professor, engrossed in the delicate work of removing a bullet from his patient's lung, listened to the message sent to him from the nearby police station, and gave a satisfied grunt behind his mask. Some time later, as he was handing over the last of the stitching to his registrar, another message was relayed to him; he thanked the nurse who had given it to him, stood while his smock was untied and went out of the theatre. A moment later those still in it heard him laughing as he went along to the changing-room.

Jane spent her afternoon tying up the last of the presents, gossiping with Bessy, presiding over her tea party, conferring with Annis about the next day's meals and taking the cats and dogs for a brisk walk, and after tea by the fire in the sitting-room she took herself upstairs to change for the evening. Should she wear the blouse and skirt again, she wondered, or the green cashmere? She could tuck a scarf in the neck and wear the brown kid court shoes which had been so shockingly expensive. She went downstairs presently, well pleased with her appearance, and sat down in the small easy-chair she had clearly claimed for her own. The wall sconces were sufficient to light the room dimly and she forbore from turning on the lamp on the small table beside her. The firelight was sufficient. A pity she couldn't see herself but, as far as she could judge, she made a pretty picture for anyone coming into the room. The anyone being Nik, of course.

Her heartbeat quickened when she heard the car whisper to a standstill. The dogs rushed to the door as he opened it and he bent to fondle them. His, 'Hello, Jane,' was quiet, as he crossed over to his chair.

'Have you had a busy day?' she wanted to know. 'Dinner's in half an hour, but Annis can delay it if you would like that.'

'Half an hour is fine. What have you done with your day, Jane?'

'I drove to Amsterdam and did some shopping. There are a lot of narrow streets there, aren't there? I—I took a wrong turning and went down a one-way street but such a nice policeman stopped me and told me to follow him—he went with me as far as the very edge of the city.' She added airily, 'I wasn't sure if I should give him a tip, but perhaps he was just doing his duty...'

The professor smiled, not very nicely. 'He was doing what I asked him to do. Fortunately I am fairly well acquainted with the traffic police stationed by the hospital. It seemed good sense to get you out of Amsterdam before you caused an accident.' He added gently, 'I saw you from the hospital.'

'Oh... I thought...' Jane paused, struggling not to let him see how awful she felt. 'I'm sorry to have been such a nuisance. I won't go out with the Fiat again, not until I know my way around.'

'I am relieved to hear you say that. I would have disliked having to forbid you to drive alone.'

She sat up very straight. 'You sound like a Victorian husband.' Her voice shook with temper.

He shrugged his shoulders. 'Possibly—I am also a law-abiding citizen intent on keeping his wife out of the courts.'

'Well, really!' Jane's eyes flashed green fire. 'I am not a child.' In contradiction of this she got to her feet. 'I have a headache. I think I'll go to bed.'

'Dinner?' enquired her husband mildly, getting up to open the door.

'I'm not hungry.'

She swept past him and he put out a hand and halted her, to drop a careless kiss on the top of her head. 'Crosspatch,' said the professor.

She undressed and had a bath and got into bed, trying not to think about the *canard avec sauce bigarade* that Annis had prepared and cooked with such care. There was a *compote* of fruit to follow, rich with brandy. Jane ate a dry biscuit from the tin on the side-table, punched up her pillows and opened her Dutch grammar.

It was Bessy who came after an hour or so, carrying a tray laden with covered dishes. 'Well, I've never known yer 'ave an 'eadache in me life before,' she observed briskly, 'but if the professor says it's an 'eadache then an 'eadache it is. A light meal, he said, so Annis and me we've put our 'eads together.'

She arranged the tray across Jane's knees and took off the covers. A meal to delight Lady Grimstone, thought Jane, surveying the spoonful of scrambled egg on its small square of toast, the little bowl of bouillon, the baked custard flanked by a glass of tonic water. She thanked Bessy, told her that it was just what she fancied and assured her that her headache would be gone by morning. When her faithful friend had gone she gobbled up everything on the tray, snivelling and sniffing like a small child.

She hated him, she told herself; he was nothing but a tyrant, and marrying him had been the greatest mistake of her life. She paused to contemplate life without him and was forced to admit that, tyrant or no, a future without him would be dust and ashes.

She pretended to be asleep when Bessy came back for the tray but she was still awake when the professor's firm tread signalled his way to bed. He didn't pause outside her door. 'Heartless beast,' muttered Jane into her pillows.

The morning saw her looking, even if not feeling, normal. She bade him good-morning over the breakfast table in the friendliest manner and began to tell him about the Mothers' Union tea party—she stretched her account to its utmost length, aware that he wanted to read his letters, but was too well mannered to say so. She waffled on for some minutes and then said with an air of contrition, 'I'm sorry, you're anxious to read your post,' and then sat, eating her toast with a wistful air, being elaborately quiet.

The professor, watching her from lowered lids, wondered why it had taken him so long to discover that he loved her—and, now that he had discovered it, it was probably too late to tell her. She had never shown any sign that she considered him more than a friend with whom she had entered into a sensibly arranged marriage. Her elborately staged little scene in the hall he had put down to boredom. He sighed. Sooner or later she would meet a man of her own age.

As he got up from the table he said mildly, 'Don't forget that we are going to Hilversum this evening—the hospital reception.'

'Will you be home for tea?'

'Unlikely. It starts at seven o'clock. I'll do my best to be here by six—get Grimbert to lay out my dinner-jacket, will you?' He paused by her chair and she looked up at him, smiling, but all he did was pat her on the shoulder in an avuncular fashion.

She walked down to the village later to have coffee with another of the professor's friends; a nice old lady, living alone except for a housekeeper as old as she was, and a bad-tempered poodle. The old lady was forthright. In fragmented English, helped by arm-waving and odd words Jane had begun to pick up, she gave it as her opinion that it was high time that Nik had married. 'There have been van der Vollenhoves in that house since your William and Mary; he needs sons to carry on the name.'

Jane, faintly pink, murmured agreement.

She gave a good deal of thought as to what she should wear for the evening, taking out the three dinner dresses and trying them on in turn. In the end, with Bessy as an enthusiastic audience, she decided on the pale coffee silk, its round neck just right for the pearls and the tiny sleeves just covering her shoulders. There was a darker velvet coat with a dramatic fullness to go with it and high-heeled silk slippers.

'You look a treat,' Bessy assured her.

The professor was of the same opinion when he got home, although he couched his admiration in somewhat more formal terms, adding that perhaps she had better have her Christmas present then and there since it would complete her outfit: pearl and diamond drop earrings in a delicate filigree design.

Jane caught her breath. 'Oh, Nik, they're beautiful, thank you very much.' She hooked them into her ears and turned to face him from the mirror, smiling with delight.

'You like them? They were my great-grandmother's. When we have the time we must get the rest of her jewellery from the bank and you may choose what you wish to have.'

She kept the smile on her face with an effort. The earrings were lovely but he hadn't chosen them, only given her what she supposed a succession of van der Vollenhove wives were entitled to.

She said simply, 'Thank you, it was most thoughtful of you to give me these.' She put up a hand to touch the earrings in turn. 'I'll take great care of them.'

He went away to his room and presently drove her to Hilversum and the hospital.

The professor knew everyone there, of course, and after the formal greeting from the director he took her arm and introduced her to a succession of rather grave gentlemen and their dignified wives. They were all kind to her and she was conscious of Nik's solid person, elegant, faultlessly dressed, his handsome head towering above everyone else there; beside her, his hand on her arm, reassuring.

There was no dancing, just standing around drinking the excellent champagne and eating delicious morsels, and when the *burgemeester* had left the more senior members of the hospital left too. Jane was quite reluctant to go for she had struck up an acquaintance with several of the younger wives, but, armed with invitations to coffee and drinks sufficient to last well into the New Year, she got into the car beside Nik.

As the car slid away into the dark he said, 'I'm proud of you, Jane—you were quite the most beautiful woman there.'

'Thank you, Nik, but it's the clothes. Your friends were all very kind.'

'The annual ball at Amsterdam will be a very grand affair. Utrecht holds what I believe is called a *soirée* but they are both in the New Year.'

They dined together in the friendliest manner but as soon as Nik had had his coffee he pleaded work to do and disappeared into his study.

Jane, ever hopeful, sat by herself, turning the leaves of a book and not reading a word. When ten o'clock struck she bade Bruno and the cats goodnight—Daisy was with her master, of course—and went upstairs to her room. She had thought once or twice that evening that Nik...but no, he had presented the correct picture of a newly married man, that was all.

She woke early, her head filled with ideas—she needed to do something outrageous, something to make him notice her—see her as someone other than the convenient wife he had acquired. Until now, she had fulfilled her role adequately, she considered. True, there had been the unfortunate episode in Amsterdam and perhaps she had been unwise to encourage Wilber, although she had done it in the most discreet and matronly fashion.

She got dressed and went down to breakfast and found Nik already at the table, immersed in his post. She wished him a cheerful good-morning, begged him not to get up and sat down. Presently she said brightly, 'I have some very last-minute shopping to do. I think I'll go to Amsterdam this morning.'

'I shall be going there after I've been to Hilversum.'

'Oh, that's no good at all,' she told him briskly, 'I shall go as soon as I've seen to the dogs and Simpkin and Percy. I want flowers, lots of flowers for the house and some more baubles for the tree. Grimbert found a boxful but there aren't nearly enough.'

'Grimbert may drive you to Amsterdam . . .'

'He's taking the Fiat to Utrecht to have a tooth out.'

The professor put down his letters. 'I'm afraid you will have to forgo your shopping, Jane.'

'There's another car in the garage.' She smiled at him and swept her eyelashes up so that her eyes were very wide open. 'A Bristol.'

'Indeed there is. Understand me, Jane, you are not to drive alone until I have the time to go with you and make sure you are capable.'

Which remark was all she needed to make up her mind. She said sweetly, 'Yes, Nik. I do understand you.'

'Good.' He got up. 'There's a backlog of work to get through before Christmas. I shall be late home.'

'I shall decorate the tree,' Jane told him, the very picture of a good wife.

With Grimbert safely out of the way, Annis consulted about dinner and Bessy instructed about the animals, Jane, dressed tidily in the Burberry skirt, a cashmere sweater and the suede jacket and wearing her sensible shoes, went round to the back of the house, opened the garage door and inspected the Bristol, noting that the petrol tank was full. For one moment she feared that there would be no ignition key and there wasn't, then she remembered where the keys were hidden in the boot-room behind the kitchen. There was no one about; she hunted around and presently found them in the toe of a wellington boot. She had to take all three back to the garage since they were unmarked and, having found the right one, go back yet again to put the other two back into the boot. It was a small setback and she had counted on being in Amsterdam well before midday, but since Nik had said that he would be back late she still had all day and since she had told Bessy that she would be out for lunch no one would be any the wiser.

Only this time providence wasn't as kind. She found the Bristol easy to drive and her confidence grew with each mile, slightly dimmed by the knowledge that Nik, if he ever discovered what she had done, would be angry. She had never seen him angry but she suspected that it would be an occasion to remember. She was driving circumspectly round Waterlooplein when she glanced sideways from her window. The Bentley, with the professor at the wheel, his face so grim that she felt sick and her hands shook on the wheel. He was looking ahead but as she peeped quickly, he turned to look at her. Only a few moments ago she had wondered what he would be like if he were angry—now she knew. She gulped down fright, saw a narrow street to her right and turned into it, thankful that the stream of cars prevented him from following her.

She had taken care to con a ground plan of the city this time and although she wasn't exactly sure where she was she knew the direction she was taking. Besides, she could see the vast outline of the hospital ahead of her and it was close by it that there was a car park. She drove carefully, keeping an eye open for the Bentley, but there was no sign of it as she parked the car in a corner nicely sheltered by a high wire fence. A study of her map showed her where to go in order to reach the shops and she set out on foot.

She had made her purchases and was within sight of the hospital, making for the car park, when she felt the ground rocking gently under her feet. She stood still, as did everyone else on the street, and then, as the ground surged violently, someone screamed. A moment later she watched the row of small warehouses on the other side of the street slowly disintegrate and slide down on to the pavement. People in the street began to run, shouting to each other, and she nipped into a doorway, afraid of being swept away by the sudden tide of humanity. The ground beneath her feet heaved gently once more and she watched in horror as a tall building between her and the hospital looming behind it swayed, chunks of masonry and concrete raining down around her. People were still running, making for a small park she remembered passing, but after a minute or so, the ground once more stable under her, she started off in the direction of the hospital, not five minutes away.

It took longer than that though for the streets were blocked by debris and broken glass and people, taken by surprise, still running to and fro. When she did get there she was taken aback to be stopped by a policeman.

She said in a voice she strove to keep steady, 'I must go to the hospital, my husband is there.'

He was a nice man, calm and patient. 'English? Not permitted...'

'He's a surgeon there—a consultant...'

He shook his head again. 'Only those with wounds may enter.'

He patted her shoulder and a cloud of dust arose; she hadn't realised that she was smothered in it. She lingered, hoping that he might change his mind, wondering what she should do next. The hospital looked all right from where she stood but there was debris all over the place; there might be damage inside, Nik might be hurt. There were ambulances now and a trickle of those with minor injuries. She looked at the police officer again but he shook his head just as he was joined by another policeman on a motorbike.

Jane recognised him at once. 'You must help me,' she told him, clutching at his sleeve. 'Remember me? Barones van der Vollenhove?' She had never called herself that; it sounded strange in her ears but it might help. 'My husband, you know him—Professor van der Vollenhove, I must go to him. I am a nurse and I can help. They'll need all the help they can get for a bit.'

She watched the man sort out her words. 'You are a nurse, *Barones*?'

'Yes. Trained in a London hospital, and you do remember me?'

'*Ja, zeker.*' His station had good reason to remember the professor; he had operated upon the commissar's small son when he had been at death's door, and only last week he had found a bed for one of the traffic policemen's wives. He said something to his colleague and said gruffly, 'Come with me, *Barones*.'

There was a great deal of broken glass, for the hospital windows had been shattered, and there were odd bits of brick and stonework lying around, but they picked their way across the forecourt to the side-wing which housed the accident department. There was a good deal more damage here and a wide path was being shovelled free from glass and bricks so that the ambulances could get to and fro. There was a steady stream of people too; flying glass had taken its toll.

At the open door, the police officer left her, muttering something in Dutch and at the same time giving her a gentle push forward. The place was crowded but she edged her way in, peering into cubicles as she went looking for Nik, terrified that she would find him lying unconscious on a trolley.

She saw him finally with a great upsurge of relief, stitching up a long gash in a boy's arm while an elderly man—a porter, she presumed—made an effort to sweep away the broken chairs, shelves and their containers, and glass mixed with plaster from the walls.

Jane took off her jacket and hung it on a convenient piece of wire sticking out of a wall, took the broom from the elderly man with a smiling nod towards the stream of people still coming in, and began to clear up.

The man went willingly; probably he thought that she had been sent to relieve him, and she didn't waste time wondering about it. She worked her way round her oblivious husband, clearing a space round the trolley.

He was standing ankle deep in glass. 'Move your feet, Nik,' said Jane briskly. For a moment she thought he hadn't heard; he tied a neat knot in the gut, snipped it and turned to look down at her.

She couldn't understand what he was saying, which was perhaps just as well, but she could see that he was labouring under some powerful emotion. He said in a cold quiet voice, 'How did you get here?'

She was feeling a trifle light-headed; the earthquake had been a nasty experience and she had spent what had seemed like a lifetime wondering if he had been injured, killed even. She said pertly, 'I asked a policeman.'

She smiled at him from her dusty face and began to wield her broom once more, to such good purpose that she felt free to look around for more useful work. Coming in now were what seemed to be an entire infants' school, howling and screaming, dirty, bewildered and terrified.

Jane handed her broom to a man standing nearby in a cloth cap. '*Schoonmaak*,' she told him, remembering that useful word from Annis and her housekeeping. She smiled into his surprised face and began to make her way towards the children. As she went she thought she heard the professor laugh but it seemed unlikely.

Nobody asked who she was or what she was doing there; they were too glad to have an extra pair of hands, sorting out the children who needed attention and those who were uninjured. She was kept too busy to see what Nik was doing but she could hear his voice from time to time and presently she saw him striding away out of the department with a young doctor at his heels. She was holding a small boy while a houseman cleaned and dressed the cuts on his leg, and she watched him, hoping that he would see her. He had never, in fact, lost sight of her; now he looked across at her, an unsmiling glance which left her shaken.

She had no idea of the time but she longed for a cup of tea. The flow of frightened people was slowing to a trickle, there was order out of chaos now and other hospitals in the city were taking over. She was bandaging a teenager's cut foot when one of the doctors who had been helping said, 'You are a stranger here? Not Dutch?'

'English—I'm Professor van der Vollenhove's wife.'

The young man looked alarmed. 'He knows that you are here?'

'Oh, yes.' She added casually, 'I expect he is in Theatre.'

'Yes—a glass splinter in a woman's chest—very nasty.' He added awkwardly, 'We are indebted to you for your help. You would like to go to the professor now?'

'He'll send for me,' said Jane and thought it very unlikely that he would do any such thing. She was wrong.

She was buttoning the last of the children into his coat when she was tapped on the shoulder. 'Professor van der Vollenhove wishes you to go to his office. I am to take you there, *Barones*.' The nurse was young and had a cheerful face and a nice smile. 'You will wish to wash your face?'

Jane wasn't tired, she was too young and healthy for that, but the prospect of Nik's controlled anger was daunting. A clean face might help to restore self-confidence. She followed the nurse to a small cloakroom, where she surveyed her appearance with horror. A dirty, dusty face stared back at her from the looking-glass; she washed it and combed the worst of the dust out of her hair and wished she had some make-up with her. Somewhere in the accident department she had a jacket and a shoulder-bag; she supposed she would have a chance to find them later. She found the nurse waiting for her, obviously anxious that no time should be wasted. The lifts weren't working on that side of the hospital—they toiled up several flights of stairs before crossing a wide landing to the central building. Here she was led through a swing door and down a wide corridor—the theatre unit, she guessed, seeing the swing doors at the end. Halfway down the nurse stopped and tapped on a door with the professor's name on it, opened it and stood aside for Jane to go in.

The room was quite small with a tall narrow window, a large desk with a swivel chair behind it, another chair facing it and rows of shelves, crammed with books. It was empty.

Jane went to the window to look out, feeling deflated; going through the hospital, she had busily boosted her morale ready for Nik's questions and anger, but now it was all oozing away again. The door behind her opened and he came in, still in his theatre gear, and the sight of him sent every single reply she had rehearsed so carefully right out of her head.

He said blandly, 'Do sit down, Jane. Someone will bring us some tea in a moment.'

So she sat in the chair opposite the desk and he sat down, picked up a pen and began to write, saying as he did so, 'Forgive me, but this is a report which must be sent at once.'

A nursing aide brought a tray of tea and he said, 'Please pour, Jane—I'm sure you will be glad of a cup.'

She poured and the cup rattled in the saucer when he asked her with a kind of cold politeness, 'Where did you leave the Bristol?'

She put the cup and saucer down because her hand was shaking. 'In the car park on the other side of the hospital. On the right-hand side at the back against a high wire fence.'

He nodded and picked up the phone and spoke into it. 'If you will let me have the key, it can be fetched here.'

'The key.' She took a mouthful of tea; it might give her a bit more courage. 'Oh, yes—the key. Well, actually it's in my shoulder-bag and that's with my jacket hanging on a piece of wire sticking out of a wall in the accident department.'

He took this information without a quiver, merely picked up the phone once more, and spoke into it. Before Jane had finished her tea the same nurse who had brought her to the professor's office arrived with her jacket and shoulder-bag. The professor thanked her nicely while Jane, feeling at a disadvantage, scrabbled around for the key. She found it as the porter tapped on the door and came in. It was a pity that she couldn't understand Dutch, she reflected, listening to the brisk interchange between Nik and the man, who took the key and disappeared. She would have to have lessons. Hard on the thought came the doubt as to whether there was much point in that; Nik would be far better off without her. She poured another cup of tea with an unsteady hand. She said in a voice which held only the faintest wobble, 'I expect you are very angry,' and when he didn't answer, 'I didn't know that there would be an earthquake—I mean it's not the sort of thing you would expect in Holland, is it?'

'Indeed not,' agreed her husband. He had finished his writing and was sitting back at his ease, watching her. Indeed, his stare began to make her uneasy so that she said sharply, 'You don't need to stare, I got a bit dusty...'

She picked up the teapot again for something to do and set it down with a thump when he asked pleasantly, 'Why did you do it, Jane?'

She didn't pretend to misunderstand him although she had been dreading that very question. It would have to be answered and she supposed the sooner the better. It was strange how a few words would without doubt alter her life...

'Well, it's like this—I know it sounds silly but I wanted to make you notice me—so that you'd look at me twice and not just now and again if you see what I mean. I can see now that it was a stupid thing to do—it wasn't going to make any difference.'

She took a gulping breath. 'I did it because I'm in love with you and I wanted you to fall in love with me.'

The professor got to his feet and she had the impression that he was a lot nearer to her than he actually was, and at the same moment the phone rang. Whatever he had intended saying would have to wait. He uttered some forceful Dutch and lifted the receiver. A moment later he was at the door on his way out of the room. All he said was, 'Don't go.'

Jane sat down again. Left alone, she had ample time to regret every word she had said. Nik couldn't ignore them and she had placed him in an awkward position—he would have to find some way of glossing over her silliness. What was she going to say when he came back? Make a joke of it? Pretend that she hadn't said any such thing...?

There was a tap on the door and the porter came in with the Bristol's keys and handed them over to her with an, '*Alsjeblieft, Barones.*' They were a means

of escape, a sign from heaven, she didn't stop to think
where she would go, or of the consequences, just to
get away from that cold stare ... !

She shook the worst of the dust off her jacket and
put it on, picked up her shoulder-bag and took the
keys. She hesitated a moment, wondering if she should
leave a note, but since she had no idea what to put
in it she rejected the idea, opened the door and peered
cautiously into the corridor. There wasn't a soul in
sight which was a good thing for the door was some
way off. Every nerve on edge, she reached the door
and opened it carefully. The professor coming out of
the theatre doors at the other end of the corridor was
just in time to catch a glimpse of a russet head of
hair.

There was a wall phone close by; he picked it up
and spoke at some length into it then went back into
the theatre to tell his registrar that he would be at
home if he was wanted urgently. Then he went on to
the changing-room. Five minutes later he emerged,
immaculate, unhurried and apparently without a care
in the world, to go to his office, cast an eye around
to see if Jane had left him a note, and then to make
his way down to the reception hall.

Jane, clutching her car keys, reached the vast hall
without mishap. She was almost at the entrance doors
when one of the women clerks sitting at the row of
desks along one side of it stopped her with a smiling,
'Excuse me—Barones van der Vollenhove? You have
been helping during the emergency this afternoon? If
I might have one or two particulars?'

She had stationed herself in front of Jane so that
she could see the whole of the reception area and Jane
could see nothing but the girl's polite face.

'Is it necessary? I do want to get home as soon as possible.' Jane paused to add, 'What very good English you speak . . .'

'Thank you, *Barones*, we are taught it at school. If you could tell me at what time you reached the hospital? After the earthquake? During the earthquake?'

'Oh, after it, I was too scared to move before then.'

One question followed the other and some of them Jane thought privately sounded silly, almost as though the girl was making them up as she went along—as indeed she was. A resourceful young woman, she was relieved to see the professor's massive form coming towards them. 'Well, thank you, *Barones*,' she said finally. 'I'm sure that's all I need to know.'

Jane said goodbye and put an eager hand on the doorknob.

'No,' said Nik very quietly in her ear, and put a hand over hers. He took the key gently from her too, opened the door with his other hand and swept her outside. It was quite dark by now for the afternoon had been lost in the rush and the panic of the earthquake. It was very cold too, and an odd flake of snow drifted down as he pulled her to a gentle halt.

'At least there are no telephones here,' he said, and sounded as though he was laughing. 'Were you running away, my darling? Will you listen to me first?'

Jane was intending to get away as far away as possible from the things her impetuous tongue had said. 'I am not running away,' she told him crossly, 'and I won't listen, why should I?' and then, remembering his words, 'What did you say?'

'I asked you if you were running away, my darling, because if you are it will be of no use for I shall come after you wherever you go.'

'You will?' She gazed up at him in the sudden blaze of light as someone switched on the powerful lights over the porch.

'Oh, yes. I have been trying to think of a way of telling you that I love you to distraction but you see I have been in mortal terror that you would quote chapter and verse of my reasons for marrying you—and that would have served me right...'

'Indeed it would.' She thumped his waistcoat. 'You were so angry when you saw me in the Bristol...'

'Angry? I could have wrung your neck, my dearest heart. You're no more fit to drive through Amsterdam than a baby is to push its pram. My God, darling, I have never been so terrified...'

It was hard to imagine him terrified of anything. 'Really terrified?' she asked. 'Just because I was driving...?'

He said, suddenly grave, 'Yes, Jane.'

'Then I won't drive in Amsterdam again.' She remembered something then. Her eyes glued to his tie because she couldn't face that blue stare, she said. 'You called me darling—was that because I told you that—well, because I said what I did just now in your office?'

He wrapped his great arms around her. 'I think that you have always been my darling only I never realised it—why else should I badger Lady Grimstone to give you a job and why else should I beard terrifying matrons in remote hospitals?'

'One matron,' she sighed into his shoulder. 'I didn't think you liked me very much.'

'Like you? Like you? My dearest heart, I may not have known that I loved you at first, but you were always in my heart and mind, someone I wanted to know better, to be with.'

'Yes, but...' began Jane, and was hushed.

'We are wasting time,' said the professor and bent his head and kissed her. A long, gentle kiss. He sighed and kissed her again—it was no longer gentle but very satisfying.

Jane looked at him then and said, 'I'm so glad we're married, Nik.'

He ran a gentle finger down her cheek. 'So am I, my darling.' She thought he sounded as though he was laughing again. 'We're going home.'

With his arm around her, they left the circle of light and began to walk towards the Bentley in the darkened forecourt, much to the disappointment of the reception clerks, the head porter and sundry hospital staff, who happened to be in the entrance hall and who had been a delighted audience.

Dear Reader,

Betty Neels is a unique and much loved author, and you will know that she uses some medical settings.

If you enjoy stories with a medical flavour, featuring a variety of countries and different medical disciplines, and peopled with characters as heartwarming as those created by Betty Neels, why don't you look out for the

— MEDICAL /\ROMANCE —

series, which publishes new stories each month for your pleasure and entertainment?

Wishing you happy reading.

The Editor

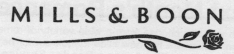

Next Month's Romances

Each month you can choose from a wide variety of romance with Mills & Boon. Below are the new titles to look out for next month, why not ask either Mills & Boon Reader Service or your Newsagent to reserve you a copy of the titles you want to buy – just tick the titles you would like and either post to Reader Service or take it to any Newsagent and ask them to order your books.

Please save me the following titles:	Please tick	√
THE WEDDING	Emma Darcy	
LOVE WITHOUT REASON	Alison Fraser	
FIRE IN THE BLOOD	Charlotte Lamb	
GIVE A MAN A BAD NAME	Roberta Leigh	
TRAVELLING LIGHT	Sandra Field	
A HEALING FIRE	Patricia Wilson	
AN OLD ENCHANTMENT	Amanda Browning	
STRANGERS BY DAY	Vanessa Grant	
CONSPIRACY OF LOVE	Stephanie Howard	
FIERY ATTRACTION	Emma Richmond	
RESCUED	Rachel Elliot	
DEFIANT LOVE	Jessica Hart	
BOGUS BRIDE	Elizabeth Duke	
ONE SHINING SUMMER	Quinn Wilder	
TRUST TOO MUCH	Jayne Bauling	
A TRUE MARRIAGE	Lucy Gordon	

If you would like to order these books in addition to your regular subscription from Mills & Boon Reader Service please send £1.80 per title to: Mills & Boon Reader Service, Freepost, P.O. Box 236, Croydon, Surrey, CR9 9EL, quote your Subscriber No:................................... (If applicable) and complete the name and address details below. Alternatively, these books are available from many local Newsagents including W.H.Smith, J.Menzies, Martins and other paperback stockists from 10 September 1993.

Name:...

Address:...

....Post Code:............................

To Retailer: If you would like to stock M&B books please contact your regular book/magazine wholesaler for details.